Friend or Foe?

✪   ✪   ✪

Sam followed Buffalo Bill's gaze to the front door, where a bearded giant had just entered. In his hand, the man carried a heavy club. In his eyes, there was a scary glint. Sam had seen the man before on the streets of Paradise Mountain. He was not the kind of man one forgot.

The bearded giant made his way to Sam's table. People got out of his way—everybody seemed to know who he was. The man sat beside Bill. He laid the club on the table, and regarded Sam with a glance that sent shivers up the bounty hunter's spine. Had Sam gotten lucky and found the killer he sought already?

Also by Dale Colter

The Regulator
Diablo at Daybreak
Deadly Justice
Dead Man's Ride
Gravedancer
The Scalp Hunters

Published by
<small>HARPERPAPERBACKS</small>

DALE COLTER

THE REGULATOR

PARADISE MOUNTAIN

HarperPaperbacks
A Division of HarperCollinsPublishers

HarperPaperbacks *A Division of* HarperCollins*Publishers*
10 East 53rd Street, New York, N.Y. 10022

Copyright © 1992 by HarperCollins*Publishers*
All rights reserved. No part of this book may be used or reproduced in any manner whatsoever without written permission of the publisher, except in the case of brief quotations embodied in critical articles and reviews. For information address HarperCollins*Publishers*,
10 East 53rd Street, New York, N.Y. 10022.

Cover illustration by Miro

First printing: June 1992

Printed in the United States of America

HarperPaperbacks and colophon are trademarks of HarperCollins*Publishers*

❖ 10 9 8 7 6 5 4 3 2 1

PARADISE MOUNTAIN

⊛ PROLOGUE ⊛

THE KILLER PAUSED AT THE HEAD OF THE pass. The frigid wind made a low, whistling sound as it whipped through the ponderosa pines and craggy ledges of the mountains. Huddling against it, the killer tugged up the collar of his mackinaw.

Above him, the lowering clouds had built up in layer after heavy layer. The sky had turned milky white, until it seemed that it was almost bursting with snow. The killer was lucky. He had just beaten the storm. Much later, and he would have been cut off in the mountains. He had been fortunate to get through as it was. Previous storms had already left the snow deep in places, too deep for wagons to pass. The storm that was about to break looked like it would be the worst of all. After this, the mountains might be cut off until spring.

Below him, a stream wound its way through the mountains. Straggling up the pine-covered slopes on both sides of the stream was a mining camp. Though it was early afternoon, lights winked throughout the camp, yellow pinpoints in the premature dusk caused by the approaching storm. The smoke of a hundred fires curled into the air, to be borne away by the wind.

The killer stretched his stiff back in the saddle. He had ridden long and hard, using up horses the way some men went through cigarettes. He had taken great pains to cover his trail. No man alive could have followed him; he was certain of that. He had done his job, and now he was finished. He was looking forward to a hot bath, a bottle—and a woman.

At the thought of the woman he wiped the back of his mouth with a gloved hand. Then he kicked his horse and eased him down the pass, toward the mining camp. As he did, the first flakes of snow began to fall.

Behind the killer, at the head of the pass, was a crudely lettered sign, erected by one of the first miners to venture into this inhospitable country. The sign read:

WELCOME TO PARADISE MOUNTAIN

CHAPTER 1

THE DRIFTER WANDERED FROM SALOON TO saloon, along the twisting lane that formed Paradise Mountain's main street. Every second structure on the street seemed to sell liquor. The remaining buildings were supply stores, restaurants, and groceries, though most of these were closed or boarded up tightly for the winter and abandoned.

The mining camp was a collection of timber shacks and half tents lining the street and dotting the surrounding mountainsides. There were no sidewalks, and the drifter moved cautiously. Bottles, tin cans, and broken boxes were half-frozen into the deep slush, along with piles of

animal droppings, making the footing treacherous. From the crowded saloons and dance halls
came the music of fiddles, punctuated by the
harsh laughter and shouts of men, and the
higher-pitched, more brittle tones of whores and
hurdy-gurdy girls.

The drifter turned into the next saloon, a
place called Charley's, and he made his way to
the bar. Business in the saloon was slow at the
moment. One of the two bartenders, a cheerful
fellow with a waxed mustache and brilliantined
hair parted down the middle, sidled over to him.

"What'll it be?" asked the barkeep, revealing
teeth and gums blackened by scurvy.

"Whiskey," said the drifter.

The barkeep filled a glass from a keg of
house whiskey. He pushed it across to the
drifter, who tossed some coins onto the rude
pine bar.

"What is this, about the seventh night in a
row you been in here?" said the barkeep, by way
of conversation. "You're almost a regular."

"Not much else to do when you're snowed in,"
replied the man. He spoke in low, measured
tones, but there was a timbre to his voice—a
menace—that made the listener take notice. "I'm
waiting for the weather to break so I can move on.
Tell me, you seen any other strangers in town?"

The barkeep thought. "Nope, none I've
noticed. Not many come through here in the
winter."

"Big fellow, he'd be, maybe flush with money?"

"No. Ain't seen nobody like that. Why'd you ask?"

"Just wondering. Looking for an old friend. Thought I might find him here. He owes me some money."

"You low on money?" said the barkeep.

"I've seen flusher times. You know where there's any work to be had?"

The barkeep shook his head. "Not in Paradise Mountain. The mines is shut down for the winter, and everything else is closed up tighter'n a nun's ass. I'll be lucky to keep my own job, the way things is going. We don't get food up here soon, the whole town's liable to close. Hell, we might go to eating each other—that's how bad it is."

"Mm," the drifter murmured assent. "My hotel's halved its meal portions, and they weren't too big to start with." He finished his drink and the barkeep poured him another, taking a coin from the bar.

The barkeep looked around, but there were no customers deserving his attentions, so he turned back to the drifter, ostentatiously polishing the bar as he spoke. "Yes, sir, flour's worth its weight in gold right now. Lot of boys that chose to winter up here are wishing they hadn't. Ain't been a food shipment in two months."

"A long time," said the drifter, sounding surprised in his low-key way. "The weather hasn't been bad that long. What happened?"

"Who knows?" said the mustachioed bar-keep. "I hear some shipments got hijacked in the mountains, but that's just rumor. All I know is, there ain't been none. Now the snow's come, and there's no telling when they'll be able to get food to us. These boys got money, and nothing to spend it on but whiskey."

The drifter mulled that over. "If things looked so bad, why didn't more men go below when they had the chance?"

"Didn't want to get their claims jumped. There's good diggings hereabouts, but if they leave, they'll lose them. Hell, they're losing them either way. Don't a week go by, some of the boys don't get run off—or worse."

The drifter was about to ask the barkeep what he meant by that when a noisy crowd of miners came in, and the barkeep went off to serve them. The drifter turned and leaned against the bar while he watched the crowd. He seemed nonchalant, almost bored, but if one looked more closely beneath his battered hat, they might have noticed his eyes, which were at odds with his bearing. The eyes were ice blue— killer's eyes—and they searched the crowd care-fully, methodically, missing nothing.

The drifter was tall and lean, with a long, much-broken nose. He wore a wool plaid coat and a scarf over layers of sweaters. His usual footgear was knee-high Apache moccasins, but now he wore well-greased leather boots against the cold. His dirty-blond beard had been allowed to grow, both by the necessities of the trail and to hide the fearsome scar that ran from his left ear to the corner of his mouth—a scar by which he might be recognized.

The drifter's name was Sam Slater, though some called him "The Regulator." He was a bounty hunter, and right now he was hunting a killer.

A wealthy merchant named Ed Robinette had been murdered in Tucson, his head smashed in by a heavy instrument. Robinette was an ex-miner, a man who'd started with nothing and made himself rich. Distrustful of banks, he was known to keep large amounts of cash and valuables in his house. The house had been systematically ransacked by his killer, and everything of value taken, including a strongbox filled with jewelry and important papers—which the killer no doubt intended to open at his leisure.

Robinette's bereaved family had put up a reward of two thousand dollars for the killer's apprehension—all the money that they could scrape together—along with the promise of another thousand for the return of the papers and valuables. Sam Slater had been passing through Tucson at the time of the crime. The money had sounded good, and Sam intended to collect it.

Robinette's killer had not been seen, but he

had left tracks. Sam had started after the man, but taking him had not been easy. The killer had traveled fast, changing horses frequently—stealing them, killing their owners when he had to, so as not to leave witnesses. He had used every trick to cover his trail, but Sam had stayed with him for four hundred miles, across the desert, through the foothills, and into the mountains. The man's trail had led him to Paradise Mountain. Sam had arrived a week ago, half-frozen, in the midst of a raging blizzard. At that, he counted himself fortunate not to have died in the bleak mountain passes. He was certain the killer was still in the camp. No one—except maybe for Sam—could get out in this weather. He had to find the man before the snow melted and the passes reopened.

Sam didn't know what the killer looked like, but he knew from his tracks that he was heavy-set, probably Sam's own height or taller. Still, that description could fit a quarter of the five hundred or so men in town—miners were brawny by the nature of their work. Sam knew one other thing about Robinette's killer. Among the items taken from the dead man's possession had been a watch—a silver Seth Thomas timepiece with Robinette's name inscribed on the back. As far as Sam knew, that watch was still in the killer's possession.

Sam finished his drink and placed his empty glass on the bar.

"Another?" said the barkeep.

Sam waved him off. "Got to meet somebody." Sam moved away from the bar. He was glad to leave. In this last week he'd consumed far too much rotgut for his liking. He'd breathed in the stench of tobacco smoke and vomit and unwashed men until it made him sick. He preferred the clean, outdoor life—the kind of life he had lived while an adopted member of the Apaches, or before that, in Montana. But it was not to be. He had chosen his path; now he must go where it led him.

He pushed open the saloon's heavy door—no batwing doors in the high country—and stepped into the freezing night. He had been cultivating acquaintances among the camp's lower element, hoping they might lead him to Robinette's killer. He was supposed to meet one of these men—a fellow called Buffalo Bill—tonight, at a Saloon known as the Through Ticket.

He made his way down the slush-filled street to the Through Ticket. The saloon was a log shack, with an elk's antlers spread above the front door. It was more crowded than Charley's. Inside, a fiddler essayed "The Irish Washerwoman" with a limited degree of skill.

Sam went in.

CHAPTER 2

INSIDE THE SALOON, MEN WERE JAMMED shoulder to shoulder, drinking, playing cards, talking. The fiddler could barely be heard above the din. A few whores circulated, now and then leading a man outside, to their cribs on the Line. Leftover Christmas decorations hung forlornly on the saloon walls, the pine needles turning brown, the colored ribbons faded. At the bar and the gaming tables, men paid with gold dust, coins, and occasional greenbacks—which were not considered as valuable as specie and were therefore heavily discounted.

Sam wrinkled his nose against the blue haze of tobacco smoke, and against the sour-onion odor of sweaty bodies. He felt his skin prickle, and he unbuttoned his coat at the oppressive heat that filled the building.

He steered his way to the bar and got a drink. He sipped it, peering at the crowd through the smoke. The men in the bar were a good cross section of the camp. Most were miners, but there were also drifters, men on the run, merchants, freighters, even a cowboy or two, snowed in for the winter. The babble of languages and accents took in every state in the Union and half the countries in the world. There were no Chinamen or blacks, though—they were not allowed.

At last, Sam found the man he was seeking—a stocky fellow with the heavy-lidded gaze of a bully. They called him Buffalo Bill because of his shoulder-length blond hair; Sam didn't know what his real name was. The man saw Sam at the same time and pushed toward him.

"Been waiting for you," Bill told him. "Cold out there, ain't it? I hate this goddamn weather. Wish to hell they'd found all this gold in the desert somewhere."

Sam grunted noncommittally. He noted that Bill's teeth were not in the same bad condition as most of the camp's inhabitants, and that he managed to look well fed despite the shortage of food.

"Buy you another drink?" Bill asked.

"I won't say no. My poke's running low."

Bill got them both another whiskey. He brought back the glasses, then led Sam to a nearby table. There were three miners at the table, but they got up and left when they saw Bill coming.

The two men sat, and Sam got to the point. "You tell your friend about me?"

Buffalo Bill nodded. "He's coming to meet you."

"Has he got anything for me?"

"He'll tell you." Bill slugged down his drink and looked around. "He should be here by—here he is now."

Sam followed Bill's gaze to the front door, where a bearded giant had just entered. In his hand the man carried a sawed-off baseball bat. In his eyes there was a scary glint. Sam had seen the man before on the streets of Paradise Mountain. He was not the kind of man one forgot.

The bearded giant made his way to Sam's table. People got out of his way—everybody seemed to know who he was. It was the same reaction that Sam had seen on the streets. The man sat beside Bill. He laid the baseball bat on the table, and he regarded Sam with a glance that sent shivers up the bounty hunter's spine. This man fit the size for Robinette's killer, and that bat could have produced the ferocious damage Sam had seen inflicted on the dead man's skull. Had he gotten lucky and found Robinette's killer already? He would need proof, if he had—a confession, or Robinette's watch, or the strong-box with the dead man's papers.

"Hi, Johnny," said Buffalo Bill. Bill was tough enough, but he was ready to bow and scrape to somebody tougher. "This here's the fellow I been telling you about. Name's Sam. Sam, this is Johnny Egan."

Sam nodded. Without taking his eyes off Sam, Egan said to Bill, "Get us a drink."

"Sure, Johnny," said Bill, and he rose and hurried to the bar.

"What's your last name?" Egan asked Sam.

Sam forced himself to meet the big man's chilling gaze. "Whatever suits you," he replied evenly.

Egan grunted. "I seen you around. Been here about a week, ain't you?"

He didn't miss much, Sam thought. "About that."

"Drifting through, or on the run?"

"Could be one, could be t'other. Could be they're the same."

Egan mulled that over. He looked like a man who could explode at the least provocation. Bill returned with a bottle. Egan refilled Sam's glass, then drank from the bottle himself. "Bill tells me you're looking for work."

"That's right."

"What kind of work you do?"

"Whatever's around," Sam said.

"The job I'm thinking of could get a little rough."

"How rough?"

"Shooting, maybe. That bother you?"

"Long as I ain't the one that gets shot," Sam said. "How's the pay?"

"Real good, if you do the job."

"Which is?"

Egan reached forward and poured Sam another drink. "You'll find out when the time comes."

"And when is that?"

"Soon enough. I've got to talk to the boss about you first."

"Sounds pretty mysterious to me," Sam said.

"It's just smart business. The boss don't like to have his affairs noised about."

"Who *is* the boss, anyway?"

"That's for me to know. You just take the money, if you're hired, and don't ask questions. How do we know you're any good? How do we know you ain't just talk?"

"Well, I ain't got references, if that's what you mean," Sam told him. "Anybody that could fit that bill is dead. Come to it, how do I know *you're* any good?"

The giant's heavy brow darkened. For a moment Sam thought he was going to reach across the table and hit him. "See this bat?" Egan said, pushing the sawed-off baseball bat toward Sam. "See them notches?"

Sam looked. Rows of notches had been carefully carved along the bat's tapered handle.

Egan went on. "There's a notch for every head I've cracked with this bat." His dark look subsided and he smiled. "Now, I ain't sayin' that every man I've hit has died, but most of 'em have. The rest sure as hell had some powerful headaches." He laughed, and Buffalo Bill laughed with him.

Sam rolled the bat over appreciatively, examining it. Several of the notches were recent, and he wondered if one of them represented Ed Robinette. "How many notches you got on here, anyway?"

"You know, I ain't counted lately. They been comin' so fast." Egan laughed again. Again Bill laughed with him.

Sam and Buffalo Bill nursed their drinks while Egan laboriously counted the bat's notches. "Forty-eight, forty-nine," he concluded. "Forty-nine, I got."

Bill said, "Pity it ain't an even fifty, huh, Johnny?"

"You know, it is that," Egan replied, drinking from the bottle again. "Well, that can be fixed. I'll have fifty tonight, or I'll know the reason why."

He looked around the crowded saloon. His gaze came to rest on two men just entering—a compact, muscular old man with a white beard, and his companion, a slightly taller black man. Egan frowned. "Sure, and I told that nigger not to come in here again."

The two miners stood at the bar. Egan rose, taking the bat with a smirk. "Watch this."

He sidled innocently through the crowd toward the two men, the bat dangling from his right hand. Sam's gut tightened as he realized what Egan was going to do. He was going to kill a man—for no other reason than to get another notch on his damn bat.

Egan wormed closer to the unsuspecting miners, who were laughing at the bar. Sam's brain raced. This was not his affair. If he interfered, he could ruin his chances of finding Robinette's killer. He could ruin his chance at finding out who the "boss" was. He didn't want to tangle with Egan. Still, he couldn't stand by and watch a man killed.

He got up and started for the bar.

"Sam . . ." cautioned Buffalo Bill, but Sam paid him no attention.

Egan was near the two drinkers now. A few men had noticed him and drawn out of his way, giving him room. He moved behind the black man. With a swift, smooth motion he took the bat in both hands and raised it behind his head. As he began his downward swing, Sam stepped forward and pulled the bat from his hand.

Egan whirled, furious. "What the . . . !" Behind Egan, Sam saw the black man and his companion turn. He saw the looks on their faces as they realized what had almost happened to them.

Egan's huge nostrils flared. "What did you do that for?"

Sam hefted the baseball bat. "It just didn't seem fair, what you were doing."

"It was none of your damn business, what I was doing. Now, give me that bat."

"When you cool off," Sam told him.

"You'll give it back now, or you won't be alive when I cool off."

Sam tapped the bat in his palm. "Then I guess you'll have to take it back—if you can."

Egan held aside his coat, to show that he was not wearing a pistol. "I ain't armed."

Sam tossed the bat aside, and it went skittering along the sawdust floor. "Neither am I, now."

All around, men scrambled out of the way. The fiddler stopped playing and dived behind the bar. The black man and his partner stood transfixed.

Egan's teeth flashed through his bushy beard. His piggish eyes came alight. "You just made yourself one big mistake, mister." He assumed a fighting stance. "I'm thirty-two years old, and I ain't never been beat in a fistfight."

"Who you been fighting?" Sam said. "Women?"

Roaring, Egan swung a huge fist. Sam ducked under the blow, hearing it whistle above him. He drove his own fist into Egan's gut. The big man let out his breath with a whoosh, and Sam followed with a left to the jaw that staggered Egan back into the bar.

Egan was strong, though. As Sam moved in, the big man shrugged off the blows. Backhanded, he threw a bottle at Sam from the bar top. Sam ducked it, and as he came back up Egan hit him solidly on the cheek.

Sam's eyes watered from the force of the blow. Egan followed with a punch to Sam's stomach. Sam doubled over. Bile rose in his throat. Before he could recover, Egan clubbed him on the temple, knocking him down.

Sam shook his head, trying to get up. Egan grabbed him by the coat collar, lifted him, and ran him across the room into the saloon wall. Sam put out a hand at the last minute to keep from hitting his head. He crashed off the wall and sank to the floor.

Egan moved in on him again, kicking him. Desperate, Sam raked the floor with his leg. His boot caught Egan's ankle, tripping him. The big man lost his balance and fell. That gave Sam a chance to crawl away. He staggered to his feet, his mouth still full of sour-tasting bile.

Egan advanced with a bull-like rush. Sam hit him two shots on the jaw, but it was like hitting a side of beef and had about as much effect. Both men circled, breathing heavily. Egan swung; the pile-driving blow caught Sam above the left eye, drawing blood. Sam responded with two shots to Egan's gut. Egan swung again, rocking Sam alongside the head. Sam gave him two more hits to the body. He couldn't match the big man's strength. Bust him up inside, that was his only chance. Another exchange—one shot to the head, two to the body—then they drew apart. Both men were breathing hoarsely, sweating, burning like furnaces in their heavy coats. Egan's face was red from his exertions. He moved in again, swinging both fists. Sam ignored the heavy blows, concentrating on the big man's stomach. One, two, three, four, he hit Egan in the gut. Egan held on, smashing Sam's face, grabbing him and trying to chew off his ear. Sam forced himself not to think of the pain, to concentrate on Egan's belly, which he pounded mercilessly. The force of Egan's punches began to fade. He grunted with pain at each of Sam's blows. One of Sam's punches lifted the big man up onto the tips of his toes. Again and again Sam hit him. Egan was no longer fighting now, just holding on. Sam drove one last punch into Egan's breadbasket, then stepped back. The big man teetered, stumbled backward, and fell heavily against the saloon wall. He slid down, coming to rest on the floor with his back and head propped against the wall. He leaned to one side, moaning. Blood trickled from his mouth and nose.

Sam stumbled across the room. He lifted one of the wilted Christmas wreaths from the wall. He came back and dropped the wreath over Egan's head. Blood from the cut flowed into

Sam's eye, obscuring his vision, as he looked for his hat. Someone handed the hat to him—he thought it was the black miner's elderly partner, but he wasn't sure, because of the blood in his eye and the way the room was spinning. His stomach contorted in pain. His head rang like a church bell. His oft-broken nose wasn't damaged, though—he could hardly believe it. It felt like the only part of his face that was still in one piece.

He put on the hat, straightened with an effort, and walked from the saloon. Buffalo Bill watched him but made no effort to help him or to intervene in any way.

Outside, Sam took three steps up the street toward his hotel, then he collapsed unconscious in the dirty snow.

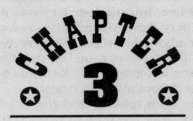

CHAPTER 3

SAM OPENED HIS EYES.

He was inside a one-room house. He was in bed, warm, under layers of blankets. He smelled broth and cheap perfume. He smelled the soft scent of a woman. He must be in a whore's shack. He doubted if there were any "decent" women in a camp like Paradise Mountain.

It was late night or early morning; he saw darkness through the drawn curtains. He heard the chill wind whistle through chinks in the wall. A fire crackled nearby.

He tried to move, and he groaned.

"How do you feel?" asked a husky voice.

With painful effort Sam looked over. He saw

a woman of about thirty. She might once have been attractive, but now her face was drawn and hard, leathery beyond its years. A long, unsutured scar above her right eye gave further evidence of the hazards of her profession. In addition, the left side of her face was lumpy and swollen, as if from a recent beating.

"Awful," Sam replied, and the word sounded like it came from the bottom of a deep well. "My head feels like a Chinese gong."

The woman laughed, revealing the same scurvy-blackened gums as the rest of the people in town. She wore a heavy shawl over a frowzy dress and fishnet stockings. Layers of cheap jewelry adorned her neck, ears, and wrists.

Sam touched the cut above his eye and felt a heavy bandage.

"Couldn't afford to send for the doc and get you stitched," the woman apologized. "Guess your eye's going to look like mine. You want a drink?"

Sam nodded.

The woman poured two glasses of brandy. She helped Sam sit up in the creaky bed. Waves of pain crested over him. He sipped the brandy, and its raw fire revived him.

He looked around. Besides the bed, the shack's main furnishings were a stove, a battered chest, and a handmade chair. "How did I get here?" he said.

"I found you in the street, after the fight. I

got Karl and Frenchy—those are the two fellas that almost got whacked in the Through Ticket—to carry you here."

"Does anyone else know I'm here?"

"I don't think so. I tried not to be too obvious about bringing you."

"Good." Sam sipped more of the brandy. He didn't like to be indebted to anyone. "You didn't have to do this."

She coughed, a deep, consumptive cough acquired from years of breathing in tobacco fumes and drinking cheap whiskey. "Listen, I'd do anything for the fella that beat up Johnny Egan."

Sam smiled, a gesture that brought him pain. "You don't like Egan?"

She turned the swollen left side of her face toward him. "Are you kidding? The bastard beat the hell out of me last week. Celebrating, he called it."

"Funny way to celebrate."

The woman snorted. "Johnny's a funny fella. He can't perform—man-wise, if you know what I mean—so he makes up for it with his fists."

"Did you know that before you went with him?"

"Every girl on the Line knows it, but it's business. I can't afford to be choosy about my customers. Once I could have, maybe, but not now."

Sam spilled a drop of the brandy. He went to wipe it off with the back of his hand, and he realized that his face had been shaved.

The woman saw the look that came over him. "I had to take off your beard," she explained. "It was full of blood. Sorry."

"That's all right," Sam said. "I didn't like it much, anyway."

"Guess you grew it to hide that scar, huh?"

"Something like that."

The woman suffered another coughing spasm. The coughing was so deep, she had to pause and catch her breath. At last she said, "That's a rough scar. How'd you get it—if you don't mind my asking?"

For a moment Sam was back on that moonlit night in Montana, watching his drunken uncle struggle atop his sixteen-year-old cousin, Lucinda, watching him tear at her clothes. He heard Lucinda's screams, the screams that had brought him from his alcove room in the barn. His reaction to the sight had been instinctive.

"I got it trying to help somebody out of a tight spot," he told the woman.

"Kind of like you did tonight, huh?"

"More or less."

Sam remembered how his uncle had come at him with the knife, slashing, insane with drink. He remembered defending himself, reluctantly at first, then with violent rage after his face had been sliced open. He remembered gutting his uncle with his knife, and what his uncle's body had looked like afterward. He remembered his cousin Lucinda's screams and the strange feel of his cheek flapping against his jaw. He had been branded for murder for killing his uncle. He was still a wanted man in Montana. It was on that night that he had begun his life of wandering.

"My name's Laramie, by the way," said the woman.

"I'm Sam."

"Sam what?"

"Just Sam."

"All right, Just Sam." She grinned at him. It was amazing how she could be so cheerful with the kind of life she must lead.

Sam returned her grin, weakly because of the pain. He said, "How'd you get a name like Laramie? You born there, or something?"

She shook her head. "Laramie's where I got my start in the game. That was a long time ago. I never use my real name, I hardly even remember it. My mom started me. We needed the money I brought in."

"She in the business, too?"

"Yeah. I never knew who my father was. I don't think Mom did, either."

Laramie poured them more brandy. Into hers, she added a few drops from a small vial.

"Laudanum?" Sam guessed.

The woman blushed through her pale, drawn face. "It helps. I started a couple years ago, to ease the pain from an abortion. I sort of kept at it, after. Occupational hazard, I guess you could call it."

Sam changed the subject. "Johnny Egan, has he been in town long?"

"Since last summer, when the rush started. That's pretty much when we all came, except for the fellas that first found the gold."

"Has Egan been out of town in the last couple weeks?"

"I don't know. I ain't seen him, but then I don't look for him, so that don't mean much. I try to keep out of his way."

"Do you know who he works for?"

"Works for himself, far as I can tell. He's usually flush with money. Steals it, I guess."

"What was he celebrating the night he beat you?"

"Whatever it was, I wasn't dumb enough to ask him about it. He beats you bad enough when you're on his good side. Why all the questions about Johnny Egan, anyway? I seen you sitting at that table with him. I thought you and him were friends."

Sam shook his head. "I just met him."

"Then that fella he was going to hit with the bat—you're *his* friend?"

Sam shook his head again. "Nope."

"Then why did you get involved?"

"Seemed like the thing to do at the time."

Laramie coughed again, and when the coughing was over, she sipped her brandy greedily. "Well, I'm damned."

"We may both be, before this is over."

Laramie turned to the small stove. "How 'bout some broth?"

Sam realized how hungry he was. "That'd go down real good, Miss Laramie."

She ladled pale liquid into a chipped porcelain bowl. "It's mostly water, with some salt pork in it. I been boiling it off since I brought you back here. Here's a crust of bread to go with it. Not your basic down-home meal, but it's the best I can manage at the moment."

"I'm sure it's excellent," Sam said.

Laramie spoon-fed him the broth. As she did there was a knock at the door. Sam wondered if Egan knew where he was, but before he could caution Laramie, the door opened, and a sharp-featured man wearing a plaid Scots cap poked his head in.

"Sorry, Laramie. I didn't know you had company," said the man.

"Yeah, well, the next time try knocking, why don't you? I ain't so hard up for trade that a little politeness wouldn't be appreciated. It ain't like you're one of my regulars, or nothing."

The man's tiny eyes studied Sam for a moment, and something like shock crossed his face, to be quickly dismissed as he turned back to the woman. "Sure, Laramie. Like I said, I'm sorry. How 'bout tomorrow night?"

Laramie looked at Sam, then back at the man. "I don't know, Willie," she said, in a voice dripping with sarcasm. "I'll have to check my appointment book. See me then."

The man nodded, and with a last glance at Sam he closed the door.

When he was gone, Laramie laughed. "Fancy that. A real paying customer, and I got to turn him away."

Sam said, "My money belt's in my trousers. Let me give you something for—"

"Don't even think about it. I ain't a charity case yet. I told you, I was glad to do it."

Laramie coughed and drew the heavy shawl more tightly around her shoulders. She spooned some more broth into Sam. "What brings you to Paradise Mountain, Just Sam?"

"Passing through. Looks like I could have picked a better time to do it, though."

"You can say that again. This town is going to hell in a handcart. Has been ever since Harry Hastings got here."

"Who's Harry Hastings?"

"The Hastings Mining Company. His operation is further up the mountain, you can't see it from here. He got here at the beginning of the fall, set up a quartz mill, or a stamping mill—I don't really know what you call it. Mining ain't my strong suit. All I know from the boys is, there's a big vein that runs through Paradise Mountain, and Hastings wants it all. He's been buying up claims, diverting water away from the other claims for his own use."

"What if the miners don't sell?"

"They get their claims jumped, or they have 'accidents.'"

"Is Hastings behind that?"

"If he is, nobody can prove it. One way or the other, though, he ends up with the claims."

"Can't the law do anything about it?" Sam said, though after a week's stay in the camp, he could already guess the answer to that question.

Laramie snorted, "What law? Tom Jeffcoat and his 'police force' are hired guns, working for the saloon keepers and gamblers. They're here to keep the boys from raising hell about the crooked card games and the watered down drinks. That, and to keep people like me in line. Tom can't see further than the bottom of a faro box. He knows as much about mining as I do, and that ain't much."

This was interesting, thought Sam, but he had his own problem, which was finding Ed Robinette's killer. The troubles of Paradise Mountain were not his concern. The camp would have to look out for itself.

By the time he had finished his broth, gray dawn was breaking in the valley. he sat up slowly on the side of the bed. "I better be going."

Laramie looked down at the floor, shyly. "You know, you can . . . you can always stay here if you like." For a moment Sam had a glimpse of the girl she must once have been.

"Thanks, Miss Laramie, but I best get back to the hotel. I've got to get a change of clothes." He motioned to the chair, where his bloodied shirt and undershirt hung.

She helped him stand. "I'm all right," he said, wincing.

"I could get your clothes for you," Laramie said. "I could drop these with Won Lee. He runs the laundry. He'll get them as clean as—"

"Thanks," said Sam, stretching out the kinks, "but there's something else I've got to get from the hotel."

"What's that?" she said.

"My guns."

CHAPTER 4

LARAMIE HELPED SAM PUT ON HIS BLOOD-stiffened shirt and his coat.

"I'll walk with you," she said.

"You don't have to," Sam told her.

"I don't *have* to do anything. It's a free country. I guess I can walk with somebody if I want."

Sam looked at her. Her eyes were more hollow than ever. "You stayed up with me all night," he said, just realizing it himself. "You haven't gotten any sleep."

"I got all day to sleep," she replied. "Besides, after I put in all this time on you, I got to make sure you're all right, don't I? I don't want you passing out in the snow, maybe freezing to death. You wouldn't be the first that's happened to, you know."

Sam relaxed. He realized there was no arguing with her. "All right."

Laramie put on her own coat, a threadbare garment of cheap serge, and they went outside. The morning was gray and cold, with the feel of more snow. Brooding mountains hovered around the valley, their tops lost in swirling, gray-white clouds. Pine forests poked through the snow-covered mountain sides, their branches laden with still more snow.

It was a damp cold, the kind that went right through you. Sam flapped his arms, trying to warm up. His breath turned to smoky vapor. At least the Apaches had sense enough to go below this time of year, he thought. White men would endure any adversity in the cause of greed.

Beside Sam, Laramie began coughing deeply. Sam couldn't imagine what this weather must be doing to her health, which looked none too good to start with. He took off his coat and slipped it around her shoulders. "Here, take this."

"Hey," she said, shrugging it off. "*I'm* supposed to be taking care of *you.*"

"Just take it," Sam insisted. Grudgingly, she gave in.

Laramie's shack, or crib, was one of a double row of nearly identical structures, stretching back from Main Street. The "Line," as the street was called, had a squalid, forlorn look. Trash and empty bottles were everywhere. Here and there could be glimpsed a few early risers, men on their way home, women going to the privies.

"Not exactly Nob Hill, is it?" Laramie said. Her husky voice was harsh from the coughing.

The two of them began walking, stepping carefully in the frozen snow. Laramie's thin boots didn't do much to keep out the cold and wet, and Sam took her arm to steady her against the icy footing.

"The best girls work for Steve Tracy at the Metropolitan," Laramie went on. "He keeps 'em warm and well fed—at least he did when there was still food to be had. They got bouncers to protect 'em, too." She sighed. "I used to work in a house, you know. Now I'm on my own, like the rest of the girls on the Line. I got no one to look after me. Besides my rent, I pay the marshal— who works for Tracy, by the way—fifty dollars a month to stay in business. I pay the mayor— who *is* Tracy—another fifty, plus I got to provide free trade for his friends, if they want it. That don't leave much money for me."

She perked up. "Some of 'em *do* ask for me, you know. They remember me from Denver. I was cock of the walk, then, the top girl in the top house. Boy, those were the days. I was a good looker, then."

Sam smiled at her. "You still look good to me."

"Thanks," she said, "but that's either because your eyes are bad or because you're too much of a gentleman to tell the truth. I know what I look like now. I ain't ashamed of it, neither."

They turned the corner onto Main Street. The few people who were out stared at them—the prostitute and the stranger with the bruised face and terrible scar. As they trampled through the frozen slush, Laramie slipped her arm through Sam's.

"This Tracy seems to be a big man in town," Sam observed.

"He is. Him and Harry Hastings, they just about run the place."

The street ran parallel to the frozen river. The damp, chill wind was funneled down the valley. With her free hand Laramie covered her mouth, as more deep coughs racked her chest.

Up ahead, there was a commotion. Men crowded around a shack from whose tin chimney smoke was rising. The men were ragged, marked by the effects of disease and malnutrition. They shoved and pushed for places in a rapidly growing line. As Sam and Laramie approached, two of the men began fighting, rolling around in the street, pummeling each other, tearing at each other's clothes. The others watched, more interested in defending their places in line than they were in the fight.

Sam saw that the shack was called the A-1 Restaurant. There was a hand-lettered sign tacked over the door: FRESH TODAY. DOG AND RAT MEAT. YOUR CHOICE —$10 A PLATE.

Sam and Laramie stepped around the fighters. "I told you the place was going to hell," Laramie said.

"Looks like it's just about there," Sam replied.

"It keeps the cats in business, anyway," Laramie said. "When the rats are gone, I guess we'll eat the cats."

The couple began attracting stares from the starving miners lined up in front of the restaurant. "'Morning, Miss Laramie," they called.

"How are you today, Laramie?"

"You seem popular," Sam remarked.

Laramie dismissed the compliment. "We had a fever epidemic here last summer. I did my Florence Nightingale imitation and helped nurse some of the boys. Just building goodwill for my business, you understand, though much good it's done me."

"Nursing fever patients—wasn't that dangerous?" Sam said.

She laughed cynically. "How much worse can things get?"

"If it's so bad here, why do you stay?"

"Things ain't much better anywhere else—though maybe you *can* get fresh vegetables. I ain't crazy about the idea of my teeth falling out. I look bad enough as it is. I couldn't get out till spring comes now, even if I wanted. Even then, I'll just go to the next mining camp, or the next cow town, so what's the difference?"

"Don't sound like much of a future," Sam said.

"It ain't. Hey, I been around. I know the end
of the road for my kind. Sure, when you start
you dream about meeting some nice fella and
getting married, leaving the game and living
happy ever after like in the books, but it don't
work that way. I'll never even make enough to
start my own house. Not now. I'll end up further
and further down the Line as I get older. Likely
I'll die from an overdose of morphine, or drunk-
enness, or from exposure, or being beat up.
That's if this cough don't carry me off first."

She saw Sam's face. "Don't you go feeling
sorry for me. Christ, if there's anything I can't
stand, it's—"

A bearded miner left the food line and poked
his face in front of Sam's. "Say, don't I know
you?"

Sam regarded the man coldly. "I doubt it."

"Sure I do," went on the miner. "You're Sam
Slater, ain't you? The bounty hunter?"

"The one they call the Regulator?" interjected
another, with a note of awe.

Sam said, "I told you—"

"Damn if you ain't!" said the first man, moving closer to look. "I'd know that scar anywhere.
I seed you in Lordsburg, when you brung in the
Ellison boys—or what there was left of 'em." He
turned, raising his voice. "Boys, you know who
this is? It's Sam Slater!"

There was a sudden babble of excited talk,
then the group fell quiet. The rat and dog meat

were temporarily forgotten as the men pondered what Sam's presence in camp meant.

Laramie disengaged her arm from Sam's. She stepped back. "Is that true? You're Sam Slater, the bounty hunter?"

Sam couldn't lie to her. "It's true," he admitted.

"You kill for a living," she said.

"I have killed, yes."

She stepped further away.

"Laramie, listen, I—"

"What are you doing here, Slater?" cried one of the miners.

"Who'd you come to kill?" yelled another.

A few of the men were already skulking off. No doubt they were wanted for one thing or another, and worried that the notorious Regulator might be after them.

"I'm just passing through," Sam told them.

Nobody believed that, such was Sam's reputation. There was a hoot of laughter. "Passing bullets through somebody's head," cracked one fellow.

"Well, I'm innocent," swore another, almost too forcefully. "I got nothing to worry about."

Sam had heard enough. He fixed the last speaker with steely eyes, and in a low voice he said, "Are you sure?"

The man blanched. "I'm sure. Honest, Mr. Slater, I done nothing wrong."

Sam shot his threatening gaze at the rest of the crowd, who fell nervously quiet. "I'd get back to my meal, if I was you boys," he told them.

The men returned to the line. There was no more pushing and shoving. They were careful not to look back in Sam's direction.

Sam walked away to join Laramie, who stood ankle-deep in churned up, dirty slush. He said. "Laramie, I—I wanted to tell you, but I couldn't."

"You come here after somebody, didn't you?" she said.

Sam nodded. "Yes."

"Who?"

Sam let out his breath. "A killer. I know he's in this camp, but I don't know who he is. And until I do, I didn't want him to know I was here."

This was the worst thing that could have happened. Robinette's murderer—whoever he was—would now know that the Regulator was in town. He might well suspect the reason why. He might try to get away, despite the weather. Even worse, he might try to stop Sam. And since Sam didn't know who the man was, he had to be extra careful. An attack could come from any direction.

Laramie looked disappointed. "God knows I'm no saint, but I don't hold with killing, not for money. And that's what you do, ain't it?"

"That's one way of putting it," Sam told her.

"I thought better of you, Just Sam."

Sam said nothing.

Laramie took Sam's coat from her shoulders and handed it back. Sam folded the coat over his arm, not putting it on even though it was bitterly cold.

"Thanks for your help," he told her.

She replied quietly. "Yeah. Anytime." She turned and started back to the Line.

Sam watched her for a moment, then he continued on his way.

Already, word of Sam's presence had spread through the camp. Men on the street gave him a wide berth. They grew quiet as he passed. Sam felt their stares on the back of his neck. He felt their distrust, their fear of him. They wondered what he wanted here. They wondered who he was after. They looked at him like he was the Angel of Death.

Flakes of snow drifted down. The sky was a lumpy, whitish gray. Whoever Robinette's killer was, he would be unable to escape today—and probably for some days after—no matter how good he was. Sam himself might not have survived the mountains in this weather.

The snow fell more heavily. Sam passed a butcher's shop, where another line was forming. Inside, they were cutting up mule and horse meat, though there looked to be damn little of it. Sam wondered if the horse he had ridden to town was in there, or if it had already been eaten. Beyond finding the killer, the simple problem of preventing starvation entered Sam's head. But he'd have to worry about that later.

He approached his hotel. It was a two-story

structure, made of rough logs. Sam shared a room with a half-dozen other men, sleeping on beds made of pine boards with rawhide slats and mattresses stuffed with flea-ridden straw.

Sam passed the rude table that served as a desk. The clerk and most of the hotel's guests were gathered around the sheet-iron stove in what passed for a lobby. There was no work, nothing to eat, nothing to do but try to keep warm. Sam saw the glances the men cast his way as he came in. They knew who he was, too. Involuntarily, he touched the long scar that ran down the left side of his face. If Laramie hadn't shaved off his beard . . .

Sam walked up the short flight of steps to the landing. He went down the hall and opened the door to his room. There was no lock on the door—the door was so flimsy that it wouldn't have made sense to try to lock it. A two-year-old could have kicked it in.

He walked into the room. There was no one inside, though someone had been there recently. Sam smelled freshly smoked tobacco, along with the always present odors of unwashed men and damp wool. It was a small room, with paper-thin partitions. The only furnishings were the beds. The guests stored their belongings under the beds, in the corners, or wherever they could.

Sam knelt by his bed and started to pull out his saddlebags and bedroll. Then he stopped.

His rifle was gone.

He threw his saddlebag onto the bed, but

even before he opened it, its weight told him what he wanted to know. Inside the bag his pistol belt was neatly rolled, the way he had left it. There was only one difference. His pistol was gone as well.

CHAPTER 5

SAM'S BREATH CAME IN SHORT BURSTS. Who had stolen his guns? Had it been one of the men with whom he shared the room? Another of the hotel guests? Or a casual thief, passing through the building and taking anything he found to hand? Any of these answers was possible, but Sam didn't think any of them was the right one.

His gut feeling was that he had been targeted specifically. The rest of his gear had been gone through as well, though much good that would have been to anyone. He carried his money on him, and for the rest there wasn't much more than a change of clothes. The thief had left

Sam's spare boxes of shells intact. The bastard's idea of a joke, no doubt. Whoever it was had been here just minutes before, it might even have been one of the men Sam had seen in the lobby. Sam took off his bloody shirt and put on a fresh one of checked flannel. He wadded the old one and stuffed it in his saddlebag. He'd get it cleaned later.

His bruises were beginning to ache again. He swore, both at the pain and second-guessing his decision not to carry a pistol in town. In one of Beadle's dime novels, everyone in these camps went armed to the teeth; in real life it wasn't like that—though there were exceptions. Sam had wanted to look like just another saddle bum. He hadn't wanted to draw attention to himself. He'd hoped the absence of a gun would keep him out of trouble, but he'd managed to find trouble, anyway—in spades.

He put on his coat and walked downstairs. The hotel clerk was sitting with a group of the guests around the stove. The men were talking, smoking pipes and cigars. Sam did not smell the same brand of tobacco that he had detected in his room.

The lobby fell quiet as Sam crossed. His boot heels thunked on the unfinished pine floor. "I want to report a robbery," he told the clerk.

The clerk looked up. He was surly, like most hotel clerks. It must be a quality hotel owners looked for when they hired them. The men around him edged out of the way.

"Anything of value taken?" asked the clerk, in a so-what kind of voice that announced that either he didn't believe Sam or he didn't care.

You know damn well what was taken, Sam thought. "My rifle and pistol," he said.

"Is that all?"

"It's enough. You see anybody strange around here in the last few minutes?"

"No," said the clerk. "Nobody."

"Nobody walked out of here carrying guns?"

"I told you, I didn't see anybody." The clerk turned to his companions. "How about you boys? See anybody strange?"

The other men in the lobby shook their heads. "Not me. I didn't see nothing."

To Sam the clerk said, "I'm no lawman. My advice is for you to report this to Marshal Jeffcoat."

"I intend to," Sam told him. Sarcastically, he added, "Thanks for all the help."

"Certainly, Mr. Slater." Suddenly the clerk's surly demeanor crumbled. Slater was not the name Sam had used on the register. Hastily, he added, "You don't mind me calling you that, I hope? I mean—well, I mean we all know who you really are. Now, that is."

Sam smiled faintly. He turned and walked outside.

The driving snow was so thick that he could barely see across the frozen river. Nearby, a cou-

ple of miners were pelting each other with snow-
balls, but they stopped and moved away when
they saw Sam.

Sam's first order of business was to buy
some new weapons. He was glad he still had his
money. He started down the street, keeping well
to the side, where he was partly covered by the
buildings. All his senses were alert. He knew he
was in danger, and if he was attacked, he had
no means of fighting back. Crossing streets and
alleys, he checked first, to make sure there was
no one waiting around the corner to ambush
him. Even more than before, people stayed away
from him. He might have been carrying the
plague. He almost wished that he was.

As he narrowed his eyes against the snow,
he found his mind drifting back to the woman
called Laramie. He was not a sensitive man, and
no one had ever mistaken him for one, but he
was sorry because he had hurt her. She
deserved more than that, though God knew she
must have been hurt enough in her life. She
must be used to it. Maybe that very fact was
what made Sam feel so bad.

Laramie might have made some man a good
wife, if life had worked out differently for her, if
she had gotten a few breaks. People talked
about the great opportunities to be found on the
western frontier, they talked about the freedom
and all you could do with it, but they never
talked about the bad side. For every person—

man or woman—who found success and fulfill-
ment out here, there were half a dozen whose
lives were broken, smashed, often beyond repair.
It was a cruel land, and just being strong did not
ensure survival. There was a lot of luck involved,
too. Sam knew about luck. He'd had more than
his share of it. He had survived both the mas-
sacre of his parents and that moonlight knife
fight with his uncle. He had been adopted by the
Apaches, when by all rights they should have
killed him. Then, when his Apache family had
been wiped out by the army, he had—

"Mr. Slater!"

Sam whirled, crouching. His hand dropped
to a pistol that he no longer carried, and he
cursed the lack of it. At the same time he cursed
himself for letting someone get this close to him.

Out of the snow two men approached.

Sam relaxed and straightened, as he recognized the black man whose life he had saved at
the Through Ticket last night and his older partner.

The two men were nervous at Sam's reaction, as though they expected to be shot. Then
they relaxed, as Sam did.

The old white man spoke in a wheezy voice,
with a German accent. "Ve vanted to sank you,
Mr. Slater. For vat you haff done here."

"Don't mention it," Sam said.

"I am Karl Eisenreich." The old man held out
a gnarled, swollen hand. For all his obvious

strength, he was slightly bent and arthritic, with stumps of brown teeth. He indicated the taller black man. "Zis is Frenchy."

The black man was bearded like his companion. His large, white teeth had not yet had time to go bad.

"You don't look very French," Sam observed. "Why do they call you Frenchy?"

"Had to call me something," the black man replied cheerfully. "That's the way it is when you're born a slave." Snow settled on his curly beard, turning it gray, like a theatrical prop designed to make him look thirty years older. He said, "Hadn't been for you, I wouldn't be here right now. Not in one piece, anyways."

"I told you, forget it," Sam said.

"You vould perhaps take a drink vis us?" said Karl. "Zey haff only ze viskey here, and a little beer. I am in my native Austria fond of ze schnapps, but I haff not had it in many years. I no longer can remember vat it tastes like."

"Another time maybe," Sam told him. "Right now I got things to do."

"Ah, yes. Zey say you are a great bounty hunter."

"I can't control what people say."

Frenchy said, "Well, we owe you, Mr. Slater. If there's ever anything we can do for you, let us know."

"Thanks," Sam said. "I'll do that."

The two miners trudged off and were quickly

lost to sight in the swirling snow.

Sam kept going up the street, toward a building with a magnificent sign: A. RHODES. HARDWARE AND GEN. MERCHANDISE. GUNSMITH.

Sam shook the snow off his shoulders and went inside, where it was nearly as cold as it was outdoors. A. Rhodes was not as magnificent as his sign. In the east he might have been considered handsome; out here he looked weak—a bespectacled, clerkish man. Around him were shelves full of clothes, pegs with miners' tools hanging from them, and behind his counter a series of pistols and rifles, each under its own lock and key.

Rhodes looked at Sam. He obviously knew who Sam was, and he was just as obviously scared of the tall bounty hunter with the terrible scar.

"Y-yes, sir?" he stammered.

"I'd like to buy a pistol," Sam said.

"I don't—I don't have any for sale. Not just now."

Sam fixed the man with steely eyes. He nodded his head behind the counter. "What are those? Bows and arrows?"

Rhodes looked. "Oh, those. They've—they've already been sold. They're waiting for the men to make the final payments and pick them up."

"All of them?" Sam said.

"Well, I guess some are here to be repaired, too. They don't work."

"Mind if I try one, just to be sure?"

Rhodes hesitated. "Ah, no. I'm afraid that's not possible."

"And the rifles and shotguns. I guess they've been sold, too, or are here to be repaired, or maybe they're just figments of my imagination."

"Th-that's right."

"I'll pay top dollar."

"I'm sorry." Rhodes was almost pleading. "They're not for sale."

"Who told you to say this?" Sam demanded.

"Please. I can't say. It's worth my life. Please. I don't want any trouble. I'm just a business-man."

"Sure," Sam said. "Business. Overlook any-thing else, but keep making money. That's all that counts."

Sam could force Rhodes to sell him a weapon, if he wanted to. He could smash the locks and take one, or as many as he liked. Rhodes was scared as a rabbit. He wanted noth-ing more than to bolt out the door. But it would do no good to force a gun out of him. It would probably only get the man killed, or severely beaten, for violating whatever orders he had been given. Sam didn't need an innocent man's death on his conscience.

"Thanks," he said. He turned and left. It was getting to be a habit.

There were other gunsmiths in the camp, but it would do Sam no good to go to them. He knew what the result would be. Whoever was behind this had worked quickly and efficiently. Was it Robinette's killer? Maybe, but would a common thief and murderer go to this sort of trouble? Could such a man inspire this much obedience, this much fear, in an entire town? And if Robinette's killer wasn't behind this, who was? And why?

It was time for Sam to visit the marshal, and after a week in Paradise Mountain he knew just where to find him. He headed to where the lights of the Metropolitan Saloon glowed like warm beacons through the thickly falling snow.

He entered the saloon's heavy doors. He stood to one side, letting his eyes become accustomed to the sudden brightness. He looked the room over.

The Metropolitan was full. It was always full. It featured the best liquor, the best games, the best girls in Paradise Mountain. Kerosene lamps burned on the walls, and their light reflected off the polished fixtures and the long bar mirror— Sam wondered how the hell they had ever gotten that up here without breaking it. Over in one corner was a piano, the only one in town, silent right now.

Marshal Tom Jeffcoat was in his usual spot, dealing faro bank at a long table. Jeffcoat made the Metropolitan his unofficial headquarters. He was hardly ever seen in his office or making the rounds of the town.

Jeffcoat was tall and steely-eyed, like Sam.

He had the look of a gunman, a look that Sam had seen too many times not to recognize. He had short, curly black hair and a mustache. He wore a clean shirt, a tie, and a long black coat. In the coat's pockets were the pistols that he used with such deadly efficiency. His partner, or lookout, at faro was practically a copy of himself, only blond and a bit shorter.

Sam crossed the room, eyes shifting, half expecting to be attacked by whoever it was that had set the town against him.

He stopped beside Jeffcoat. The marshal dealt another two cards—loser first, then winner. "Collect on the king," he announced. "Pay on the eight. New bets, gentlemen."

Then Jeffcoat looked up at Sam, as if noticing him for the first time, and he smiled. "Well, well. If it isn't the famous man hunter. I've been wondering when you'd show up, Slater."

CHAPTER 6

SAM EYED THE ROOM WARILY. HE HAD BEEN in hostile situations before, and he knew that he was in another one now.

At the long table next to him, the black-haired marshal looked amused as he dealt another turn of faro. "I'll collect on the two, gentlemen. Pay on the seven, this time. New bets, please."

The lookout took care of the money. To Sam, Jeffcoat said, "I was surprised to learn that you're in town, Slater." He paused. "I don't like surprises."

Sam said nothing.

Jeffcoat went on. "Been keeping a low profile,

I understand."

"I had my reasons," Sam said.

As Jeffcoat prepared to deal another turn, he idly ran his forefinger across the top card in the lacquered box. Sam knew that the card was marked with pinprick blisters, invisible to the eye. Jeffcoat could read the card with his fingertip while he studied the bets. If he didn't like the card, he would take the one beneath it, palming it out.

Jeffcoat went on. "I've heard of you, Slater. You're quick with a gun, and you're not much on bringing in your men alive. You call yourself a regulator, but as near as I can see, you're just a killer for hire."

Sam smiled thinly. "Well, you got the better of me there, Jeffcoat, 'cause I ain't heard of you. I've seen your type, though, in the Kansas cow towns and a hundred other places. You're like the Earps or the Mastersons. You do a little pimping, a little gambling, a little marshaling. If the boys complain too much about the crooked games, or the overpriced whiskey, or even about being drugged and robbed by the whores, you bend a pistol barrel over their heads or maybe you just shoot 'em. That's the difference between us. My men all needed killing. The ones you kill are drunken cowboys and miners, kids wet behind the ears and maybe away from home for the first time."

The room had fallen silent. Jeffcoat was still running his fingertip over the down card. "You're right about one thing. I worked with the Earps in Kansas. They're good men, especially Wyatt."

Sam kept smiling. "The only good stories I ever heard about Wyatt Earp are the ones he made up about himself."

Jeffcoat tapped the cards and looked up. "You didn't come here to swap insults, Slater. What do you want?"

"A little professional help."

Jeffcoat beckoned to his lookout. "George, take the deck." To another man he said, "Huey, you're lookout." He pushed back his chair and rose, indicating that Sam should move to the bar.

"Those two your deputies?" Sam asked.

"How did you guess?" said Jeffcoat.

"It wasn't hard."

At the bar Jeffcoat said, "Two whiskeys, Pete. It's on me." He rested a booted foot on the brass bar rail and leaned one elbow against the bar. The folds of his expensive black coat hung perfectly. The bulges of the pistols in the pockets were visible only if you looked hard for them. "Now," he said, "what do you want?"

Sam told him. "My hotel room's been robbed. Somebody took my rifle and pistol."

Jeffcoat sipped his drink. "I'll make a report. You got the serial numbers?"

Sam gave him a withering look. "No, and I can't recite the Gettysburg Address from memory, neither. Those weapons have my initials carved on their butts, Jeffcoat. I can recognize them when I see them. In the meantime nobody will sell me replacements. Any idea why?"

Jeffcoat looked amused. "It's a free country, Slater. People don't have to sell guns to bounty hunters, if they don't want to."

"That ain't all," Sam said. "I'm in Paradise Mountain for a reason. I'm looking for a killer, but I don't know his identity."

"And you want my help finding him?" Jeffcoat said.

"You *are* the law," Sam reminded him.

While they finished their drinks, Sam told Jeffcoat about Robinette's murder. "The man I'm searching for is big, well over two hundred pounds, and tall. He got to town eight days ago. Same day as me."

Jeffcoat studied his empty glass. "Got anybody in mind?"

"A fellow named Johnny Egan."

Jeffcoat nodded. "That's a good choice. Egan's certainly capable of that kind of crime. You got one problem, though."

"What's that?"

"Egan hasn't left this camp in four months. He was definitely here at the time you say this murder was committed in Tucson."

"You're sure?"

"I've seen him myself, here at the Met. There's Steve Tracy—ask him, if you don't believe me." Jeffcoat beckoned with a hand.

"Mayor?"

Tracy strolled over, smoking a cheroot. He was of medium height and thickly built, with the square, heavy jowls of a libertine. Diamond rings gleamed on his pudgy hands, and there was another diamond in his cravat. Tracy was a "gentleman," the kind who would shoot you to prove how cultured he really was. He was balding on top, and he combed his hair up from the ears, pomading it to keep it in place over the thin spots.

Jeffcoat said, "This is Paradise Mountain's newest citizen, Mayor. Sam Slater. Maybe you heard of him."

Tracy puffed himself up. Beneath the bombast, Tracy was a rough customer. You had to be in his line of work. "Indeed I have. Your reputation is as widespread as it is repellent, sir."

Sam said, "Then I must be in good company, between a pimp and a card cheat."

Jeffcoat straightened, moving forward from the bar, but Tracy stopped him.

Jeffcoat calmed down. Eyeing Sam, he said to Tracy, "Slater's looking for a man that got to town eight days ago. He thinks it's Johnny Egan."

Tracy unplugged the cheroot from his mouth and shook his head. "Egan's been in town for some time. I know, because I can't think of a night he hasn't spent at least some time in this establishment. He's not a welcome presence, as you may surmise."

Sam was stumped. "Did anybody get here about a week ago? Big fellow? There can't have been many come in, because of the weather. I checked all the stables, but horses are being eaten so fast, I couldn't learn anything by that way."

Jeffcoat said, "You're the only newcomer I've seen lately, Slater." He looked at Tracy, who nodded agreement.

"He's here, all right," Sam told them stubbornly. "I followed him from Tucson. He's flush with money and loot. He should be out spending it."

Jeffcoat and Tracy shook their heads.

"Anything else you want?" Jeffcoat inquired.

"No. Nothing else," Sam replied.

"Then I've got a few words for you."

Sam looked.

"Leave town," Jeffcoat said.

"I've broken no laws," protested Sam.

"You're undesirable, Slater. We try to run a nice, clean town here."

Sam laughed at that. "You mean you're afraid I'll tell the boys the card games are rigged?"

"I'm not joking, Slater."

"How am I supposed to leave in this weather?"

"That's your problem."

"And if I don't go?"

"We'll make you."

Sam grinned. "That doesn't sound like your style, Jeffcoat. It ain't like you to throw down on somebody that can fight back."

Jeffcoat bristled. "Don't press your luck, Slater. Be out of—"

"Get this straight, Jeffcoat. I came here to do a job. I'll leave when I'm finished, and not before."

Jeffcoat's eyes met Sam's. "You've been warned."

"It won't be the first time."

Sam touched his hat brim mockingly. He turned and started to walk out of the saloon.

"Slater!" cried Jeffcoat.

Sam stopped. He didn't turn. He made no sudden movements that might look like a man going for a gun. He pictured Jeffcoat standing with his hands in his coat pockets, where he kept his pistols, looking for an excuse to pull them.

"Aren't you worried that I'll shoot you in the back?" Jeffcoat said.

"I don't think even you would do that in front of a room full of witnesses," Sam replied.

He kept going out the door.

It had been a long day. Sam went back to his hotel. He walked in wearily, to find his saddlebags and bedroll lumped in front of the crude desk. The same surly clerk was on duty, this time behind the desk.

Sam indicated his gear. "What's this about?" he demanded of the clerk.

"You've lost your room," the clerk told him primly. "The hotel doesn't want a man like you staying here."

"On whose orders?" Sam said.

"The owner, of course. Mr. Cross."

"Was it his idea, or did somebody tell him?"

The surly clerk sniffed. "I don't see where that's really any of your—"

Sam grabbed the clerk by the shirtfront and hauled him halfway over the desk. "Who gave the order?"

The clerk was terrified. "I don't know. I don't know whose orders. I just do what Mr. Cross tells me."

Sam let the clerk go, giving him a little shove, so that he lost his balance and landed in a heap on the floor behind the desk.

Sam picked up his gear and left the hotel, stepping outside into the falling snow. It was almost dark now. Lights shone on the street. They glimmered in faint clusters up the mountainside across the frozen river.

Sam started walking, boots noiseless in the snow. He was right back where he had started in his search for Robinette's killer. If the killer wasn't Egan, he had no idea who it could be.

Men avoided him on the street, but he was used to that by now. He was getting more unpopular by the minute. Somebody was damned anxious to be rid of him. He needed to learn why the town was against him. He needed to learn how, or even if, that antagonism was connected with Robinette's murder, though for the life of him he didn't see how it could be.

It wasn't like he wanted to be here. This mining camp was a monument to greed. Men came here to become rich, and if they achieved that, they tried to get more. Gold had that effect. Men who might, at home, have been content with an honest income fell under the spell of gold, and no amount of it could sate their desire. It was an intoxicant, a narcotic. It kept them working when their bodies were broken by disease and malnutrition. It led them to commit acts of violence that they would never have . . .

He felt, rather than heard, the bullet whisper past his face. He dropped his gear and threw himself into the deep snow, rolling. From the corner of his eye he caught a red flash through the falling snow, followed by a muffled boom. He had no idea where the second bullet went. There was another spurt of flame, from closer by. There were two men shooting at him.

Sam scrambled to his feet and ran around the corner of the hotel. The hotel was on Commerce Street. One of the shooters was on the corner of Main Street; the other was in an alley across Commerce. Sam made for the alley at the rear of the hotel, running in the deep snow. He had to be careful not to trip over any of the half-hidden garbage in the alley. A bullet splintered the frame wall of the hotel, just behind him.

The building next to the hotel was a saloon. Sam dodged around both the back of the saloon and the next building down, which had been a restaurant but was now closed. He hoped to sneak back onto Commerce Street and catch his assailants from behind as they came after him.

He moved up the side of the abandoned restaurant, keeping to the deeper shadows of the building, though visibility wasn't more than a few feet in the darkness and falling snow. The snow stung his eyes, and he wiped his lashes clear with the sleeve of his coat.

He crossed Commerce Street, crouched low, and moved down the line of buildings on the far side. He squinted through the snow, into the street, but he saw no one. He took a few more steps. The street was empty. Whoever had shot at him had not stuck around. They had run.

Sam moved back into the shadows of the buildings, and he found the churned-up snow where one of the shooters had stood. He bent down and picked up something with a gloved hand. It was a .44–40 shell casing, already rimed with snow. Nearby was another. A caliber like this could have belonged to anyone. It could have belonged to Sam, if his rifle hadn't been stolen.

There was something else he noticed on the frigid, snowy air, so faint that he could not be sure it was even there. It was the aroma of tobacco, the same tobacco he had smelled in his hotel room earlier that day.

He followed the shooters' tracks, jogging easily in the snow, the way an Apache would. At the junction of Main Street the tracks joined another pair, then turned down the street. For all his tracking ability, Sam quickly lost them in the confusion of newly made footprints going back and forth from the saloons.

He was not far from the Metropolitan, he noted. He could go in there, but what was the use? Like Robinette's killer, the men who had shot at him could be anyone in town. Even if he did know who they were, he didn't have a gun.

Sam sighed. He went back to the street in front of the hotel and he got his bedroll and saddlebags. He pulled his collar tightly around him. Through the muffling blanket of snow, he heard the revelry of the town. The gunshots hadn't meant much to these miners. They heard gunfire every night.

Sam needed a place to stay. He thought about the stable where he'd left his horse, but if form held, they probably wouldn't let him in there. He slogged through the deepening snow to the Line. Dimly seen shadows flitted back and forth between the shacks. Lights burned. There was the sound of forced laughter.

Sam stopped outside Laramie's door. There was no sound from inside. He knocked.

After a minute the door opened. Laramie stood there, her unpinned light brown hair framed in the weak lamplight. She had the same drawn face, the same shawl around her shoulders.

They looked at each other for a moment, then Sam said, "That offer of a place to stay still good?"

Laramie hesitated, then she opened the door wider. "You know it is."

Sam stepped inside. It felt good to get out of the snow and the cold.

"I'm not interrupting you, am I?"

"You mean do I have 'company'? No. What happened to make you change your mind about staying here?"

"The marshal told me to leave town, I was thrown out of my hotel, and somebody took a shot at me. A typical day in my business."

Sam shrugged off his coat and hung it on a peg behind the door. He and Laramie looked at each other again. They were at a loss for words, after the acrimony that had passed between them earlier.

Sam tossed his bedroll against the wall. "Sorry to be a bother. I'll sleep on the floor."

Laramie sat on the bed, the covers of which had already been turned down. "No, you won't. You'll sleep here."

She held out her arms, and he went to her, though he knew that he shouldn't.

CHAPTER 7

SAM WOKE EARLY, BUT LARAMIE WAS UP first, fixing breakfast.

"How do you like your salt pork?" she inquired cheerfully from the stove, "fried, boiled, or raw and dipped in vinegar?"

Sam sat up in the rough bed. "Whatever you're having," he said.

"Then you'll get the specialty of the house. Actually, there's only about two bites of pork left, so it don't make much difference. Coffee's hot—help yourself."

Sam dragged on his clothes. Outside, the sun reflected brightly off the new-fallen snow. Inside, the little cabin was frigid. Sam rubbed his hands and blew on them against the cold. He poured some coffee and broke off a stale piece of sourdough bread. The coffee was made from oak bark, but it was black and hot.

Laramie poured her own coffee, lacing it with brandy and laudanum.

"Better go easy on that stuff," Sam warned.

She put a hand over her mouth, coughing. "I told you before about giving me orders. Besides, I got to start the day right. 'Whore's breakfast,' we call it in the trade." She sipped the coffee with a look of anticipation, and her drained face seemed to flicker to life, readying itself to face the new day.

On the small table Laramie set a plate of salt pork, which had been fried with crumbled hardtack and raisins, then sprinkled with brown sugar. "Here you go," she told Sam.

There was not even a decent serving for one person, much less two. Sam felt guilty. "I ain't hungry. You go ahead and—"

"If you don't take some of that, you'll be insulting me, Just Sam."

She was serious. Sam shook his head and spooned some of the mixture onto his plate. He poured more coffee and ate. "Hey, this is good," he told her. "You should open a restaurant."

"I ever get me a stake, maybe I will," she said, pleased at the compliment.

It didn't take Sam long to eat. "I need to borrow your gun," he told Laramie when he was finished.

"I don't have one," she said.

Sam looked at her. "How do you defend yourself?"

"Not with a gun, that's for sure. I don't believe in 'em. I seen too many people killed— good friends of mine, some of 'em. I couldn't hit that wall with one, anyway." She smiled. "Besides, I'm pretty handy in a cat fight."

"What if it ain't a cat you're fighting? What if it's somebody like Johnny Egan?"

She sipped her coffee. There was still a slight swelling around her eye from her last encounter with Egan. "I'll take my chances. Always have."

Sam felt uneasy.

"Sorry about the gun," she said.

"That's all right," he replied.

She went on. "I guess it's hard to do your job without a gun."

"It's hard enough with a gun," Sam admitted. He finished his coffee and stood. "I better be going."

She coughed again and stood alongside him. "Going where?"

He got his coat from the door peg. "I have to see a fellow. I'll tell you about it when I get back."

"Does—does that mean you *are* coming back? Here, that is?"

Sam tried to make a joke of it. "I have to. You're the only one that'll take me in."

She looked away. "Gee, thanks. You really know how to sling the compliments."

Sam went on, taking her shoulder and soothing her. "I'm also coming back here because there's no one in this town I'd rather be with. And that's the truth. There, is that better?"

She looked up at him from half-lowered eyes, pouting like the little girl she had never been. "Much," she said.

Sam ran a finger along the scar above her right eye. Then he bent and kissed her.

She touched his coat sleeve. "Be careful, Just Sam."

"I will."

He put on his hat and went out.

He left the camp by a back route, keeping his eyes peeled. The bright sun shone without warmth in a cobalt sky. As so often happened on sunny days after a snow, the temperature had plummeted. Smoke rose from every tin chimney in the camp. There were few people out.

The road to the Hastings Mine was easy to find. It started at the sandbar, across the river from the camp, then wound its way up into the heart of Paradise Mountain. The bar was where the first gold deposits had been found last summer. Men had flocked there, and the camp had sprung up around their diggings. Knowing that the gold must come from higher up, the more adventurous miners—like Hastings, presumably—had worked their way into the mountains, searching for the rich vein that produced the dust and nuggets found below.

Sam crossed the river lower down, wanting to stay out of sight. He intersected the road farther up the mountain, whose rocky peak towered above the river in the clear air. The road was narrow and winding, packed into the snow by the comings and goings of men and animals from up top. It had been graded to accommodate heavy wagon traffic, but it was now closed to wheeled vehicles because of the weather. Any materials traveling above the river had to be carried on mule back.

Sam stayed off the road, keeping to the calf-deep snow among the trees. It was safer that way. Someone had tried to shoot him yesterday, and he had no doubt they would try again, if the opportunity presented itself.

Sam climbed high into the rugged vastness of Paradise Mountain. The going was rough, but he was used to rough going. He was able to keep the road under surveillance most of the time. Every now and again he stopped, to watch and listen, and make sure he was not being followed. Once, he saw a pair of armed men coming down from above, leading two pack mules that were loaded with some kind of supplies. The men must be headed for town, but Sam did not know what they could be taking there. Gold dust would have required a larger guard, and anyway the mine wouldn't be producing gold now, not with the water supply frozen.

The morning was almost gone when Sam

spied a wooden bar across the road. On the bar was a large hand-lettered sign: KEEP OUT. Just past it was a guard shack.

The guards were nowhere in sight. They must be inside, keeping warm. Sam worked around the guard shack, on up the mountain. The road dropped over a bench near the mountain's crest, and he found himself staring down at a wide valley. At the valley's bottom was a brand-new quartz stamping mill.

The mill was an immense structure, built on five terraced levels, from the conveyor-driven ore crushers on top, to the stamps on the level below, where the crushed ore was mixed with water, to the screens on the next level, through which the mixture passed on its way to the vanners, oscillating belts that shook out the lead. What was left went into huge amalgamating pans to be cooked with mercury, and then was passed to the settling tanks, out of which the slag was taken. The remainder was gold and whatever silver was mixed with it. This operation was powered from the lowest level by three giant steam boilers. The boilers were quiet now, their tall smokestacks silhouetted against the snow. Leading from the mine shafts on the mountainside to the crushers on the mill's top floor were a zigzagging series of trestles, bearing rails along which the ore cars passed.

For a square mile around the mill, the ponderosa pines had been felled for the boilers' fuel. The tree stumps dotted the denuded mountainside, along with heaps of slag produced by the stamping process. Before the last of the gold was extracted, the whole mountain would be bare of trees.

Sam's heart was heavy at the sight. He had hunted these mountains with his Apache family, in the days before the white men had broken their treaty and driven them out. He knew Paradise Mountain, and he pictured it as it had been then—green and bursting with life. Now there was only mud and garbage and ruin. He wondered how white men could destroy the work of Ussen the Creator and call it civilization.

Sam studied the mining complex, making no attempt to hide himself. Along with the mill there were numerous outbuildings. Sheds held equipment for the mill and for the logging operation that fed its ravenous appetite. There was a siding full of ore cars. There were barracks for the employees, as well as a dining hall. Farther up the mountain—by itself, with no trestles leading to it—was a large excavation, a man-made cave. Armed guards patrolled its entrance.

It must have cost Hastings a fortune to get this operation under way, Sam thought. It must be costing a small fortune just to keep all these guards on the payroll. The guards, and there seemed to be plenty of them, were the only ones working now. When the spring thaw came, and there was water in the stream, crews would be hired to work the mill. An operation like this would use a lot of men, working in round-the-clock shifts. It could easily employ the entire population of Paradise Mountain. When that happened, the town down below would go out of business. It would move—lock, stock, and gambling hall—to the flats around Hastings's mill.

Sam shifted his perch, trying to get a better look at that strange excavation on the side of the mountain. He felt the cold creeping through his greased boots and thick socks. The wind cut through his layers of protective clothing like they were paper. This was nothing. He thought back to his days with the Apaches. One winter the Mexicans of Ures had invited his band of Bedonkohe to town to trade. The Mexicans had treated the Indians like honored guests. Old animosities had been forgotten. Food and *aguardiente* had been plentiful, especially the *aguardiente*. Then, in the night, with half the Apache men drunk senseless, the Mexicans had struck the Apache camp, killing everyone they could find. Sam had been sixteen then. He had escaped with members of his Apache family, dragging the younger children, dressed only in the clothes he had worn for sleeping. The Mexican soldiers had pursued them into the mountains. Sam remembered that time, barefoot in the snow with only a shirt and breechclout for protection, and no food to eat. He had watched men, women, and children die from exposure and starvation, but the Apaches had pressed on, with the soldiers at their backs, until they were safely hidden in the vastness of the mountains. No one had complained about the cold. No one had complained about the frostbite that numbed extremities then turned them black. Complaining was not the Apache way. Sam remembered the feel of his bare feet in the snow. He remembered the anger he had felt, his desire for vengeance. Then, as now, he had been without weapons. But during the pursuit he had killed a Mexican soldier. The Mexican had been one of the advance guards, who'd allowed himself to get too close to his quarry. Sam had ambushed the man, broken his neck, and taken his weapons and clothing. He had kept the weapons for himself; the clothing he had given to those of the band who needed it most. For that deed he had been made a warrior by the Apaches. It seemed the only profession for which he was suited.

There was a rifle shot. A bullet kicked up snow nearby. Another shot—the bullet hit in front of him this time. Sam stood straight, hands raised. Below, a trio of guards motioned him down. Two more guards came his way from further along the mountainside.

Sam walked down the mountain to the mill, hands still raised. All around, men came out of the buildings or stopped work, watching. The guards approached him, rifles leveled. They were a nasty-looking bunch, more like hired guns than workingmen.

"Who are you, and what do you want around here?" demanded a surly guard, who seemed to be the leader.

"I want to talk to Hastings," Sam said.

"Well, Mr. Hastings don't want to talk to you," the guards' leader told Sam. "We could shoot you for trespassing and be within our legal rights, you know."

"He'll talk to me. Tell him it's Sam Slater."

"I don't care if it's—"

"The bounty hunter?" said a new voice.

Sam turned to see a youngish, intense man with dark muttonchop whiskers emerge from a nearby house. "That's right," Sam told him.

The newcomer stepped off the porch, putting on his coat. Behind him, a bleached blonde watched for a second, then went back inside and closed the door.

The chief guard said, "We caught him sneaking around up top, Mr. Hastings."

Hastings waved the man off. "It's all right." He motioned toward the wooden shack that served as the company office. "Come out of the cold, Mr. Slater."

Sam went in. Hastings followed him, closing the door and straightening his expensive suit. The office was small, cramped, utilitarian. A stove in the corner kept it warm. Hastings nodded to the clerk on duty, who made himself scarce.

Hastings said, "Can I offer you a drink—coffee, whiskey?"

"Coffee'd be fine," Sam replied.

Hastings poured a cup from a pot on the stove. "I'd offer you a cigar, but I don't smoke. Can't stand the things." He handed Sam the cup. "You're something of a celebrity in the wilder parts of the world, Mr. Slater. What can I do for you?"

Sam sipped the coffee, feeling its warmth thaw his insides. "For starters, you can tell me why you're trying to run me out of Paradise Mountain."

Hastings's hazel eyes opened wide. "Me? I admit to a certain curiosity about meeting a man with your reputation, Mr. Slater. If I had children, I might even ask for your autograph. But I've never laid eyes on you. Why should I want you out of the community?"

"That's what I'd like to know."

Hastings shook his head, bewildered. "I'm afraid you've made a mistake. Tell me, why do you think it's me?"

"Who else has that much influence around here? Who could turn a whole town against me that quick? Not Marshal Jeffcoat—he never turned anything more difficult than a deck of cards. Not Tracy—he might be mayor, but his only interest is profit and loss."

Hastings cleared his throat diplomatically. "Perhaps your, ah, bloodthirsty reputation has people scared."

"Anybody without a price on his head has no reason to be scared of me."

"Well, there's no price on my head, so I guess I can relax." Hastings laughed at his own joke and added, "What brings you to Paradise Mountain, anyway, Mr. Slater?"

"I'm after a man, a killer."

"And there's a price on this man's head?"

"I don't work for free."

"Who's the man?"

"That's the interesting part. I don't know. He robbed and killed a merchant in Tucson, name of Robinette. Ever hear of him?"

Hastings shook his head. "I've never been to Tucson."

"I tracked the fellow here. He got here nine days ago, but nobody seems to have seen him—or if they have, they've been damn quiet about it."

Hastings smoothed one of his muttonchop sideburns. "I wish I could help you, Mr. Slater, but I don't get off this mountain too often. My work keeps me busy, you know."

Sam thought about the bleached blonde he had seen on the porch, and he could guess that more than work kept Hastings busy. The blonde was probably his plaything, lured away from one of the whorehouses to keep him warm for the winter.

Hastings went on. "We haven't hired any new men lately, I know that. And as you can attest, nobody sneaks up here without being seen." He smiled.

"Your boys *are* a mite touchy on their triggers," Sam acknowledged.

"They're just doing their job. They've got a lot of valuable property to protect."

"They look well fed, considering the conditions in town."

Hastings shrugged. "I take care of my people. That's one reason they like to work for me."

Sam finished the coffee and put down the cup. "What's the other reason—they like to jump claims?"

Hastings stiffened. "Who told you that?"

"I hear things."

Hastings smiled again. This time the smile was not friendly. "I buy claims, Mr. Slater, of course I do. I'd be a fool not to. I'm a businessman. I'm here to make money. That's what this country is all about, the last I heard. I buy claims, but I don't jump them." He paused. "You know, I could sue you for libel, if there were any courts in this part of the world. Of course, if there were, you'd be out of business, wouldn't you?"

Now it was Sam's turn to smile. "I'll never be out of business, Hastings. That's the beauty of my profession."

Hastings's expression indicated that the interview was over. "Is there anything else?" he asked Sam. "I'm rather busy at the moment."

Again Sam thought about the girl he'd seen on the porch. "I bet you are," he said. Then he added, "No, nothing else."

Hastings raised his voice, "Mr. Steele!"

The surly head guard looked in.

"Escort Mr. Slater off company property."

"Yes, sir," said Steele.

Sam nodded to Hastings and started out the door.

"Mr. Slater?" Hastings added.

Sam turned.

"Don't come back."

Sam fixed Hastings with his ice-blue eyes. "You know, Hastings, it's funny, but I ain't much on taking orders. Be seeing you."

Steele and the other guards led Sam down the valley, toward the road. Sam indicated the excavation high up the mountain. "What's up there, the Crown Jewels?"

"Mining equipment," Steele said tersely.

"With all those guards?" Sam said. "Who's going to steal heavy machinery in this weather?"

There was no answer.

"Friendly bunch, I'll say that for you," Sam murmured.

The silence lasted until the party reached the gate across the road. There they halted, and Steele rounded on Sam. "You heard what Mr. Hastings said, Slater. Don't come back, if you know what's good for you. Next time you leave here, it'll be in a pine box."

The guards left Sam at the gate and went back up the road.

CHAPTER 8

SAM WAITED UNTIL THE GUARDS WERE gone. Then he rounded the bend below the gate, taking a different route off the mountain than the one he had used on the way up, making his own trail. The Apaches had taught him never to leave a place the same way you came in, if it could be helped.

Sam was more convinced than ever that Hastings was behind the effort to get rid of him. He had no evidence—it was just a feeling, something in the man's attitude. But why? He couldn't figure that out. Hastings hadn't killed Robinette. He lacked the killer's large build, for one thing. Anyway, Hastings was a big-time operator; smash-and-grab household robbery wasn't his style. Hastings wasn't acting from any moral imperative in wanting Sam out of Paradise Mountain, either. Sam bet the man had no morals at all. He wouldn't have come this far in business if he had.

The afternoon was well advanced. Sam's trail dropped him into an alpine meadow, bisected by a frozen stream. Not far from where he emerged from the pine forest, there was a little gathering, some of whose members were engaged in heated argument. With a shock, Sam realized that the gathering was a funeral.

The ragged scarecrows around the grave were miners. Snow had been shoveled aside in a great pile, and the grave had been hacked out of the frozen ground with picks and axes. As Sam drew closer he saw that one of the miners held a pistol on two others—Karl Eisenreich and his black partner, Frenchy. Karl and Frenchy stood next to the body, which was wrapped in a dirty piece of canvas.

"Move away from him," the man with the pistol shouted to Karl and Frenchy.

"Ve are burying him, Charley," said Karl calmly. "Ve are Christians."

Sam came up behind Charley, moving quietly. Some of the crowd saw him, but Charley was half-crazed and did not notice their mutterings. The rest of the miners watched the proceedings with wolfish eyes made yellow by hunger.

"Move, or I'll shoot!" Charley ordered Karl and Frenchy. "Do you think it bothers me to kill you? That'll leave us with two more bodies. It'll be better for—"

Sam pulled Charley's gun hand down and at the same time twisted him around. The pistol fired into the snow. As it did, Sam brought a crushing overhand right down on Charley's jaw. The man's knees buckled, and he collapsed unconscious at Sam's feet.

Sam looked at Karl and Frenchy. "You two all right?"

"Yes," said Karl, "ve are fine."

Frenchy nodded, looking relieved.

Karl said, "Sanks, Mr. Slater. You haff done us anozer good turn. Vat are you doing here?"

"Same as always," Sam replied, "passing through. What happened?"

"Zis is George Pennington," said Karl, indicating the canvas-wrapped body.

"He die from the cold?"

"Starvation," answered Frenchy, bitterly.

Sam didn't understand. "So what's the argument about?"

Frenchy said, "Charley and some others, they want to eat him."

Sam said nothing, shifting uneasily on his feet. It was not his place to offer advice. Apaches didn't eat their dead, but Sam knew that a hungry man would eat pretty much anything. Charley was still out cold. Sam's appearance had taken the fight out of those who supported him.

Karl went on, as bitter as his partner. "Poor George. He vas living on viskey ven I last saw him. And he vas not ze only vun, by golly. It's not right. Zere is horses and mules in ze town zat could be killed, but zey belong to ze Hastings Mining Company"—he pronounced the words in mock-grand terms—"and zey can not be touched. Mr. Hastings, he keeps armed guards around zem. He says ve vill need zem, to bring in supplies and work ze mines ven ze veather clears."

"Won't be nobody left alive to bring supplies *to*," grouched Frenchy, "'cept them what works for Hastings."

"Animals is worth more than men up here," allowed another miner. "It's like bein' in the army again." That observation was followed by a rueful laugh.

Still another miner said, "I ain't had nothing to eat for two days. I'm savin' my last batch of sourdough as long as I can."

A third said, "Me, I biled my belt last night. Drank the juice, pretendin' it was soup, and sucked on the leather." He laughed a black-toothed laugh. "Best meal I had in a week."

Karl shook his head. "Frenchy and me, ve vas ze vuns zat found George. Frozen solid he vas, buried by ze snow except for a little bit. He must haff been out here for days, right vere zey left him."

"They just throwed him out in the snow,"

added Frenchy. "Didn't even have the decency to bury him."

"'They'?" said Sam.

The Austrian pointed a gnarled finger across the frozen creek. "Ze men who haff taken his claim. Zat vas his cabin over zere."

Sam followed Karl's finger to a snow-covered miner's cabin. A man lounged in the cabin's doorway, watching the funeral and holding a rifle. The man was stocky, with long blond hair. It was Sam's old acquaintance, Buffalo Bill.

"They won't let us onto his claim," complained Frenchy. "They won't even let us take care of his property. He has him a family. He may have letters for them, money even."

"Vere are you going?" asked Karl suddenly.

"Across the river," Sam said. It seemed like he was being drawn into the miners' troubles in spite of himself.

The late George Pennington's cabin was a crude affair of picket logs and canvas, its chinks stuffed none too expertly with mud and twigs. Buffalo Bill straightened nervously as Sam approached.

"Hello, Bill," said Sam. "Ain't seen much of you lately."

"I—I been busy," Bill replied, fingering his rifle.

"I can tell," Sam said. He looked around the cabin. "Never figured you for a miner."

Bill was defensive. "I done some mining. This

claim was open, so we took it."

"Any chance you might sell?"

"We might, if the right offer come along."

"You mean an offer from Harry Hastings?"

"That's none of your business, Sam. I ain't got to—"

"You got trouble?" asked a second voice, and Buffalo Bill's partner emerged from the cabin's shadows.

Sam started. The second man was Willie, the sharp-featured man with the plaid Scots cap who had come to Laramie's shack on Sam's first night there. Willie was smoking a pipe, and Sam recognized the odd-smelling tobacco. It was the same smell he had noticed first in his hotel room, and later in the street, when he'd been shot at. Willie held a Winchester rifle on Sam. The initials "S.S." were carved into the rifle's butt, and Sam had to smile as he realized that he had been shot at the other evening with his own rifle.

Guilt flooded Willie's face. He edged back into the shadows with the rifle, as if hoping that Sam wouldn't recognize it.

Sam's smile widened. "Nice rifle."

"I like it," Willie said.

"I lost mine the other day."

"Do tell."

"Had it stolen," Sam went on.

Willie tsked sympathetically. "This is lawless country."

Sam acted unafraid. He had to keep up a

bold front. There was nothing to prevent these men from shooting him. Both had him covered. The smallest move, and those nervous triggers would blast him into oblivion. Only Sam's reputation, and the fear it inspired, stayed their hands. Willie and Buffalo Bill were the type who didn't feel right shooting somebody unless it was in the back.

Willie's presence gave Sam a bad feeling about Laramie. It was a feeling he should have had earlier. He realized now that Willie's appearance at her crib that night had been no accident. Sam was worried about her safety, especially without a gun for protection. He should never have gone back to stay with her, he thought. He should never have let himself be seen with her. He knew who had stolen his things now and who had shot at him, but he would have to wait to find out why. He would have to take care of Willie and Buffalo Bill later.

He said, "The boys over there are worried about George Pennington's personal effects. Seems he had a family, and they'd like to send the stuff to them."

Buffalo Bill replied, "Tell them we'll get the stuff together and give it to them. Tell them to stay on their side of the river. They can send one man over to pick it up in an hour. We don't trust them."

Sam forced a smile. "Thanks, boys. It's been nice talking to you. Good luck with the claim."

"Sure," said Buffalo Bill, looking relieved.

Willie said nothing. He was probably wrestling with himself whether or not to shoot. Probably the only thing stopping him was his fear that Sam might be carrying a hideout gun, and that his first shot wouldn't be fatal to the feared bounty hunter.

Sam backed away from the cabin. Each step he took made it less likely that the two claim jumpers would open fire. Each step let him breathe a little easier. At the creek he turned and recrossed.

On the other bank, the body had been laid in the grave and the grave filled in. The miner called Charley had come to and left, along with many of the others. Sam wondered if they might not come back and dig up poor George later. If they did, Sam would not stop them.

Karl and Frenchy were still there. "Vat did zey say to you?" Karl wanted to know.

"Send somebody over in an hour, and they'll return the effects," Sam told him. "I'll tell you the rest later. What's the fastest way back to town?"

Karl rubbed his white-bearded chin. "Vell, you can follow zis stream. Zere is a trail, and it runs into ze river chust above ze camp. But ze fastest vay, I guess, is over zat hill and straight along, but it is hard going, and vis zis snow, I don't zink you—"

"Thanks," said Sam, and he started for the hill.

He climbed the hill, mindless of the deep

snow. He had to be sure Laramie was all right. He felt responsible for her. By the time he reached the hilltop, his thighs burned and his ankles felt like there were lead weights attached to them, but he forced himself to ignore the pain.

Before him, in the failing afternoon sunlight, he saw a series of ridges, falling away to a deep depression that must be the river valley, where the town lay, though the town itself was not visible from here.

Sam half ran, half fell down the far side of the hill, slipping in the snow, letting himself slide, bruising himself on unseen projections of rock. He crossed a boulder-strewn stream and pulled himself up the next hill, using the low branches of pines, heaving himself over sharp rocks, keeping the distant valley in his mind's eye. In this bleak wilderness there was little life. An occasional squirrel, abandoning his winter's nap in hopes of finding a pine nut, ran at Sam's coming. A crow cawed and flapped its long black wings against the rosy twilight sky.

Despite the intense cold, Sam was sweating heavily beneath his coat and layers of sweaters. Up and down, up and down he went, and each new ridge top seemed to bring the valley no closer. Sam despaired of reaching the camp, but then a stiff climb brought him in sight of the river and the winking lights of Paradise Mountain. He descended the hill into town, plowing through the snow.

The twilight had given way to a sullen gray dusk as Sam made his way into the camp. He didn't care who saw him. If someone wanted to shoot at him, let them. His legs felt rubbery and he was out of breath as he ran along Main Street and turned into the Line.

The Line was quiet at this hour. Business would start picking up later.

"Laramie!" Sam cried as he approached her shack. He was filled with a vague, nameless dread.

There was no answer. The shack was quiet. No light burned.

Sam tried the door. It was open. He stepped in. "Laramie?"

It was gloomy inside, shut up tight. He was aware of a dark lump on the floor.

Then something exploded across the back of his skull. He saw stars, and he cried out in pain. He staggered around, the pain blinding him, trying to get at his attacker. He saw a huge figure in front of him. Then he was hit again, and he knew only blackness.

CHAPTER 9

SAM CAME TO. HE WAS LYING ON A FLOOR, in the dark. His head throbbed. His vision was splintered.

Then he remembered where he was, in Laramie's house. He remembered how he had walked in and been hit. He remembered the huge figure that had loomed out of the darkness.

The pungent smell of liquor filled his nostrils. His face was covered with the stuff, wet and sticky. His right hand lay in a puddle of something else that was wet and sticky, but it wasn't liquor. It was blood. His own? No, not that much. He'd have been dead if it was.

He became aware of something on the floor next to him. A body.

Even in the dark he knew that it was Laramie.

Sam rolled onto his chest. His stomach twisted, and he wanted to vomit. "Oh, no," he moaned. He had gotten here too . . .

There was a commotion outside. Sam saw the light of torches. Someone began banging on the shack's door.

"Open up in there!" It was Marshal Jeffcoat. Sam looked around, but he knew there was no way to escape.

The door was kicked open and Jeffcoat burst in, carrying a lantern, followed by three deputies.

Jeffcoat held the lantern high. He and his deputies recoiled in horror at what they saw. So did Sam.

The interior of the house had been wrecked, as if in a desperate struggle. Laramie lay face-down, with her legs bent under her at an odd angle. Her skull had been cracked open like an eggshell. Blood and brains lay spilled across the grain sacks that served as floor carpets. More blood was splashed on the walls and furniture.

"Jesus," said the blond-haired deputy named George.

Jeffcoat looked down at Sam. "We had reports of a disturbance here. You should have left town when I told you to, Slater."

Sam struggled to a sitting position. "You don't think I did this?"

"I sure as hell do. You got a better story?"

"I been staying here," Sam explained. "I came back, and somebody busted my head. I don't know who. Laramie was dead when I got here. Why would I kill her?"

Jeffcoat looked around, distastefully. "Maybe she wouldn't put out for you," he suggested. "Maybe you did it in a drunken rage."

"I haven't had a drink all day," Sam said.

"Don't give me that. You reek of brandy."

"Whoever knocked me out must have poured it over me, to make it look like—"

"Get him on his feet, boys. Put the cuffs on him."

Outside, the crowd was increasing. The torchlight grew stronger. "What's going on?" men cried. "What happened in there?"

One of the deputies leaned out the door. "Laramie's dead. Sam Slater killed her."

There was a shocked silence. Then a roar of anger and outrage.

Sam was hauled to his feet. That act set off a splitting pain in his head. As the deputies handcuffed him he said, "If I killed her, how do you explain my head being knocked open, too?"

"She fought back," Jeffcoat said. "You're drunk, you fell and cracked your head on the edge of that table."

"You don't believe that."

"It's what a judge and jury believes that counts, not me."

"And when will I see a judge?"

"Not before spring, you can count on that."

"Here's what he done her with," said the deputy named George. With the toe of his boot, George nudged an iron poker used to stir fuel in the stove. The poker lay in the blood by Laramie's body, next to her old shawl.

Jeffcoat said, "Let's get him out of here. Huey, you stay and clean up this mess. Bring along any evidence you find."

Sam was shoved out the door. His head was beating like a Sioux tom-tom. Blood from a scalp wound trickled over the bandage that Laramie had put on him and ran into his eye, and he tried to blink it away.

Before him was a sea of angry faces, lit by torches that turned the snow atop the shacks of the Line a reddish orange. Sam thought he saw Johnny Egan among them, but in the confusion he wasn't sure. Marshal Jeffcoat led the way, carrying a shotgun. "Come on," he cried to the mob. "Make way. Make way, there. Let us through."

Two deputies held Sam's arms, guiding him because he was none too steady on his feet. The crowd surged around them. "Bastard! Son of a bitch! He killed Laramie, get him!"

Someone punched Sam. Others joined in. They hit him with fists and wooden boards. They threw things at him.

"Get back!" cried Jeffcoat. "Get back! This man is a prisoner."

The deputies held Sam with one hand, while

they tried to fend off the crowd with the other. "Get back," they told the miners, "we don't like this any better than you do."

The exhortations had no effect. The crowd made passage nearly impossible, as the little party turned from the Line onto Main Street, headed for the jail. Sam tried to duck as best he could, but blows rained down on him. Some were glancing, others were made ineffective by the miners' weakness from starvation, but many landed solidly. Sam felt blood running down his face. His ears rang.

Then he lost his footing on the ice and fell. Men began kicking him, stomping him. A painful blow to the kidney brought bile to his throat. The cold snow felt good as he lay in it. He wanted to dig deeper, to bury himself in the snow and escape the pain. He wondered if this was how he was going to die, beaten to death by a mob, for something he did not . . .

There was the blast of a shotgun.

Marshal Jeffcoat held his smoking weapon in the air. He was hatless and angry, his clothes messed up. "I said, get back! There's another barrel where that one came from."

Through swollen eyes Sam saw dozens of angry faces in the flickering light of the torches. For a second the mob backed off, but not far.

"Quick," Jeffcoat told the deputies, "get him up while we got time."

"Come on, Slater!" The deputies hauled Sam

to his feet and ran for the jail. It was hard to run in the snow and ice, with Sam only half-conscious. Before they reached the jail, the crowd closed in again. There were more blows with fists. Something hard bounced off the back of Sam's head, and he cried out in pain.

Then they were through the door and inside the building. The deputies threw Sam to the floor while they joined Jeffcoat in closing the door and barring it. Outside, the crowd raged, beating against the jail door and the front wall.

Sam lay on the floor, bloody and bruised, his clothing torn. He was only half aware what was happening. He was sore all over. He'd been pounded like a piece of tough meat.

Jeffcoat was out of breath and angry. "That was a new hat, goddammit" he said, smoothing his black hair.

"You want we should put Slater in the cell?" said the deputy called George.

"Why not?" Jeffcoat said. Cocking his ear to the uproar outside, he added, "I don't think he's going to be in there long, though."

None too gently, the deputies threw Sam into one of the cells and closed the door. They did not bother to lock it.

Outside, the crowd was yelling, "We want Slater! We want Slater! Give him to us, Jeffcoat, or we're going to come in and take him!" Sam could have sworn the last voice belonged to Johnny Egan.

Thoughts came together in Sam's battered

brain. Jeffcoat had said he'd been summoned by reports of a disturbance. But the blood on Laramie's floor had been congealing. It had been there at least an hour, probably closer to two. That meant Jeffcoat hadn't come right away. He had waited, waited for Sam to show up.

"Send him out, Jeffcoat! Send him out!"

Through the barred cell door Jeffcoat looked down at Sam, lying on the earthen cell floor in a bloody, sodden mess. "Hear that, bounty hunter? Seems you killed the wrong whore. The boys remember her for what she done for 'em during the epidemic last summer. They want her killer to pay. In a few minutes they're going to come in here, take you, and string you up. And I ain't going to try and stop them. Me and my boys ain't getting ourselves killed for you."

Sam spoke through puffed lips, spitting flecks of blood. "You're more concerned with losing your hat than saving your prisoner."

"It was a new hat. I liked it better than I do you."

"You're supposed to protect me."

"Why? You're going to hang anyway. This way the town is spared the expense of feeding you and watching you so that you don't escape."

"That's bullshit, Jeffcoat, and you know it. This is a set up, an act. That's why you left this cell door unlocked. You're just trying to make it look good so that you can say you did your best to protect me but were overwhelmed. You're trying to look like a real marshal."

Jeffcoat swung open the barred door. He kicked Sam in the face, knocking him backward. "I *am* a real marshal."

The mob was beating on the jailhouse door. "Give him to us, Jeffcoat! This is your last chance!" Sam was certain he heard Egan's voice now.

The deputies were scared. George said, "Hurry up, Tom. We've done our part. This is getting dangerous."

Jeffcoat turned away from the cell. Through the door he cried to the mob, "All right, wait!"

He and the second deputy started to unbar the door.

Through the rear window of Sam's cell, a voice called, "Slater! Get down!"

Instinctively, Sam rolled onto his face. As he did, there was a terrific explosion.

Sam looked up. The entire back wall of the jail had been blown away. The rafters collapsed in a cloud of dust and falling snow. There were cries and screams from out front.

Sam sat up. "What the—"

Before he could see what had happened to the marshal and his deputies, hands reached through the dust and debris. Coughing, two men pulled Sam up and out what had been the back of the jail, into the alley. They were Karl Eisenreich and Frenchy.

"I told you we owed you one," Frenchy said

to Sam.

Karl studied the blown-up jail with a critical eye. "Maybe chust a bit too much of a charge. Vat do you sink?"

Frenchy grabbed Sam's arm, dragging him painfully along. To his partner he said, "I 'sink' we better get the hell out of here, before those peckerwoods come after us."

CHAPTER 10

THE THREE MEN STARTED DOWN THE ALLEY behind the blown-up jail. They could not run very fast because ice and snow made the footing treacherous. The last thing they needed was for them to slip and break an ankle. Sam had to be helped along by Karl and Frenchy. Sam's hat was gone. The clothes were half-torn from his back. His face was bruised and bloodied almost beyond recognition. There was a shooting pain in his kidney where he'd been kicked. His head still throbbed from where he'd been hit in Laramie's house.

Back at the jail, all hell was breaking loose. Men were shooting, running back and forth in fright and confusion. Marshal Jeffcoat crawled from under a pile of debris, coughing, brushing dust and snow from his expensive clothes. He was surprised to still be alive. There didn't even seem to be any bones broken. There were moans as George and the other deputy emerged from the wrecked jail as well.

Jeffcoat looked around, fuming. "Where the hell is Slater?"

"He must've got away," said one awed bystander. At that moment the jail's last remaining roof beam crashed to the ground, as if to punctuate the man's remark.

Jeffcoat got even madder. "Anybody see who helped him?"

"There was two of them, I think," cried a voice. "Couldn't see who they was."

"Goddammit, I want Slater back," Jeffcoat thundered. "I want him back, do you hear? Get your guns, men, and fan out. We can't let him get away, not after what he did to poor Laramie! Five hundred dollars to the man who brings him in! Another five for the men who helped him break out!"

"Dead or alive?" shouted somebody.

"What do you think?" Jeffcoat said. "Dead."

There was a cheer, and the crowd, which had recovered from the explosion, started after Sam and his rescuers.

Meanwhile, Sam and the others turned down another alley, this one behind the street called

Dead End. Frenchy moved with athletic grace, while Karl was surprisingly spry for a man of his age and arthritic knees.

"There they are!" came a shout from behind them. "I see them!"

Sam glanced over his shoulder. Silhouetted against the snow, he saw a man at the head of the alley. The man fired a pistol to alert the rest of the pursuers. The three fugitives rounded the corner of a building, out of the man's sight. They heard his footsteps crunching the snow behind them.

Sam spied firewood piled against the building's rear. "Wait," he told Karl and Frenchy.

Still woozy, he picked up a cord of the wood. He stood by the corner of the building. As their pursuer came around the corner Sam swung the wood full force, hitting the man—whom he recognized as one of Hastings's mine guards—in the face. There was a satisfying *splat*, and the man fell onto his back.

Sam threw down the wood. He and the others kept going.

The crowd was well after them now. Sam and his friends saw the reflection of torches over the rooftops. They heard shouting. Then some fool fired a shot and that set off a flurry of confused gunfire.

Behind them, on Main Street, men dived for cover, shooting at shadows and at each other. There were cries and oaths as a few of the vigilantes were winged. Then Tom Jeffcoat worked into the melee, firing his shotgun into the air for the second time that night.

"Stop it! Stop it, you fools! You're shooting at each other! Get up and get after Slater!"

Farther ahead, Sam and his rescuers came out from between two buildings, onto Union Street. They darted across the street and went down an alley behind it. The alley ended in the snow-covered scrub at the foot of the hills. The torchlight and shouting were nearer.

Karl's gimpy knees were killing him. "I cannot go any more," he wheezed.

Badly beaten as he was, Sam needed a rest, too. In front of them was a weed-choked depression. "In there," he said.

He followed Frenchy and Karl into the bowllike depression. It was full of rusty tin cans, empty bottles and other garbage. It must have been used as a dump. Sam prayed that he didn't cut his hand and get blood poisoning as they crawled through the snow-covered refuse. They found an overhang on one side of the depression. "Here," Sam whispered. The three men squeezed through tangled brush, into the overhang. As they did, there were footsteps above them.

Torchlight shone into their hiding place. Sam and his new friends pushed back as far as they could, holding their breaths.

"See anything?" said a voice above.

"Nah," replied a second. "Nothin' down there

but some half-froze rats." The pursuers were pant-
ing, out of breath. They were probably more than
a little drunk.

"Where could they have went?" said a third
voice.

The first man said, "You want to climb down
there and look closer?"

"I don't know. Maybe we should—"

"Hey!" said a new voice. "I thought I seen
something move."

"Where?"

"Over there, on the side of the hill."

"Come on, let's check it out. And this time
don't go shooting till you know what you're
shooting at. You damn near blowed off my head
back in the street."

The men hurried off. Sam and his new
friends waited awhile, shivering under the overhang, until the first tide of pursuit had washed
over the outskirts of town and, finding nothing,
had drifted back to regroup and start again.

"Damn if I know where they could be," a
retreating voice grumbled.

"Maybe somebody else got 'em."

"Didn't hear no shooting."

The voices faded. At last Sam and his friends
rose, stiffly because of the cold, and set off.

Frenchy led them in a wide sweep around
the north end of town, then across the frozen
river and into the mountains, where they were
covered by the thick pines.

The freezing cold helped revive Sam as he climbed the mountain. He took handfuls of the snow and dabbed them on his battered face. "Where are we headed?" he asked.

"Our claim," said Frenchy.

"Aren't you afraid you'll get in trouble, taking me there?"

"Zey did not see our faces," said Karl, hobbling behind the other two with his peculiar arthritic gait. "You vill be safe vis us, for a vile at least."

Sam said, "What made you boys come to town, anyway?"

Frenchy replied, "The way you took off, we thought something must be up. We wanted to help, if you needed it."

"I'm obliged. What did you blow the jail with, blasting powder?"

"Ze prospector's friend," Karl replied. "Ve stole it from ze Hastings Company." Hastings kept a large warehouse at one end of the camp, near the river where he stored supplies for trans-shipment and the trip up Paradise mountain.

The men kept climbing, following the contours of the mountain. Below and behind them was the glow of lights from the camp. Sam, who could pick out a trail under most conditions, could find no trace of one here.

"You boys know your way around here," Sam complimented them.

"Ve should," Karl said, "I vas vun of ze first

men up here. I prospected all over zis mountain before I struck ze pay dirt."

After what seemed an eternity, they reached a stream bar. Reading the stars, Sam had an idea they were not too far from the Hastings mine. "Here ve are," Karl said.

Just up from the stream's high-water mark was a cabin. Frenchy unlatched the door and led the way inside, lighting a kerosene lamp. The cabin was more sturdily built than George Pennington's had been. The roof was made of doubled canvas, stretched taut, then painted to make it waterproof. The chinks between the picket logs had been tightly filled.

While Frenchy started a fire, Karl said, "Go ahead, Mr. Slater, haff a sleep. Ve vake you if somesing happens."

Sam was in no position to argue. He needed rest. As the fire sprang to life, its reassuring crackle provided a soothing background. The cabin's two beds consisted of canvas sacks stuffed with dried grass and leaves on cushions of pine boughs. Sam lay down on one and instantly fell asleep.

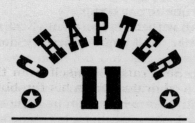

CHAPTER 11

SAM AWOKE WITH A START. INSTINCTIVELY he reached for a gun, then remembered that he had none.

Gray light flooded the cabin. The day was well advanced. Sam sat up to see Karl Eisenreich sitting on an overturned crate that served as a stool, smoking his pipe and watching him. A long-barreled squirrel gun lay across the Austrian's knees.

"Good morning, Mr. Bounty Hunter," said Karl, with a twinkle in his ancient eye. "How are you?"

"Fine," Sam replied. Actually, he hurt like hell, especially his skull, which felt like it was alternately expanding and contracting, but it was not his nature to complain.

Jabbing with his pipe stem, Karl indicated the fireplace. "Haff some coffee, vy don't you—it's real."

Slowly, Sam raised himself from the crude bed. The blood drained from his throbbing head, and he waited a second for it to come back. Then he took the coffeepot from the coals at the edge of the fireplace, and he poured some of the liquid into a dented tin cup. He sipped the coffee through lips as pulpy as if they had been stung by bees. His whole body felt like it was swollen.

Marshal Jeffcoat had been too clever for his own good, Sam thought. He should have backed off and let the mob beat Sam to death when he had the chance. They had nearly done it anyway.

Old Karl chuckled. "Vis your face zat bad, no vun vill notice your scar, by golly." He was trying to look calm, but he could not completely hide his edginess. He left his seat and peered out the cabin window, twisting his head from side to side.

"Where's Frenchy?" Sam asked.

"In ze town."

Sam drank more coffee. He had been set up last night. Somebody wanted him dead. It had to be connected with Robinette's murder. It had to be. Whoever was behind it had wanted Sam's death to look like vigilante justice. Sam had no family. No one would mourn the loss of a notorious bounty hunter like Sam Slater. No one would be likely to check into the true circumstances of his death.

And to get at Sam, they had killed Laramie. Sam remembered Laramie's smashed body in the lantern light. He remembered the huge, vaguely glimpsed figure that had knocked him unconscious.

Sam swore to himself that he would find the man who had killed Laramie. He would find the man, and he would make him pay.

There was a noise outside. Karl lifted the squirrel gun—though it would be little use against anything much bigger than a wood pigeon. He looked through the window again, then relaxed. After a second he opened the door, and Frenchy came in from the gray noon, shivering and rubbing his hands. He wore a cloth cap with earflaps.

"More snow on the way," Frenchy announced, warming himself by the fire.

"Vat is going on in ze town?" Karl asked him.

"Everybody's at Laramie's funeral. It was just breaking up when I left. The whole camp is after you, Mr. Slater. The boys is powerful worked up. They combin' this mountain."

Sam said, "Maybe I better be going."

"No," Frenchy told him. "Nobody suspects me and Karl are involved with you. They asking me have I seen you, telling me how dangerous you are."

Frenchy went on. "How about some grub, Mr. Slater? Best I can do is make you a flapjack, but I ain't got no grease to fry it with. We had some dried meat from our burro, but we finished that a week ago."

Karl shook his head. "It vas a damn good burro, too. She been vis me a long time. I hated to kill zat animal."

"I'll pass," Sam told them.

Frenchy said, "Really, Mr.—"

"It's all right. And call me Sam." Sam would not take food from starving men. He had been ten days in Paradise Mountain, and the hunger was gnawing at his gut. It never stopped. He knew what it must be like for these men, who had faced that same hunger for weeks, even months. He had been in that situation with the Apaches, more than once, and he could cope with it better than most. He thought of poor George Pennington, and of the men wanting to eat him. He wondered if things were going to get that bad before the winter ended. He was afraid they already had.

Karl went on, "Zere is food in zis camp, I know zere is. I haff seen zis all before. It's bad, very bad."

"What do you mean?" Sam said.

"Ze merchants, zey hold back ze food to drive up ze prices. Zen, ven ve are starving, zey miraculously find flour and corn." He shook his head. "Sirty years, and it never changes."

Sam raised an eyebrow. "Thirty years—that how long you been prospecting?"

"Yes, I sink so, depending vat year zis is. I haff been prospecting since ze California Rush in forty-nine. I haff seen zem all, you know— Nevada, ze Frazer River, Montana, Idaho, Colorado, Mexico—places I do not even remember anymore. I haff made fortunes and spent zem, and alvays I come back for more."

"Got the gold fever bad, ain't you?" Sam said.

"Very bad. I vould not know vat else to do. Even if I made ze big strike, I vould not stop vorking. I vould go crazy being retired, vis nosing to do but lay around vis pretty vomen to vait on me." He laughed. "You vould not believe it, but my parents, zey raised me to be a lawyer back home in Austria. Zen came ze revolution, and ze news about ze gold in California, and pretty soon I don't be a lawyer anymore."

Sam said, "How long you two been partners?"

"Since last zummer," Karl replied. "My old partner, he died from ze fever right after ve came here."

Frenchy added, "I didn't know nothin' about gold mining 'fore I met Karl. After Gen'ral Sherman 'liberated' me, I done a little bit of everything—good jobs is hard to come by for black folks, you know. I been a mule skinner, a gandy dancer, damn near anything you can think of. Anyway, I just come off a spell of mustangin', and I thought I'd try my hand at gold digging. I needed a partner, and so did Karl."

Karl said, "Zat Frenchman, he don't know much, but he is a good vorker. Smart, he is. A good cook, also."

"Yeah," said Frenchy wistfully, "I done wonders with that burro. Not much you can do with no greaseless flapjack, though—'cept grit your teeth and eat it."

Karl went on. "It vas good times, zen. All miners ve vere, here. Ve make our own rules about ze size of our claims. Ve make our own laws. You could leave gold dust in your tent and go avay for a veek, zen come back and it vould still be zere. Now, zere is a man killed here every day or so, and zey steal ze dust from under your nose. It all started ven zat Tracy came, vis his fancy girls and crooked cards, and right after him, Hastings vis his money and his mill."

Frenchy said, "It was Hastings's money got Tracy elected mayor and that cardsharp Jeffcoat made marshal."

Sam had gotten up. He hobbled around the little room, and that act started the blood flowing through his busted-up body, which set off new waves of pain. His shirt was stiff with blood. He was going through shirts like he owned the factory. "You mean it was a rigged election?" he said.

"Hell, yeah, it was rigged," replied Frenchy. "'Course they wouldn't let *me* vote, 'cause of I got me a slight skin discoloration, but everybody

DALE ✪ COLTER

we know voted for the other candidate, a fellow named Portugal."

"So what happened?" Sam said.

"Portugal had him a 'accident.' Fell down an abandoned mine shaft. The shaft was flooded, and he drowned."

"Fell or was pushed?"

"That's what a lot of us would like to know," Frenchy said.

Sam paused and looked out the window. "Well, there's somebody coming that you can ask."

French and Karl started for the window. "Who?"

"Harry Hastings."

116

CHAPTER 12

HASTINGS CAME UP THE PATH FROM THE stream, accompanied by five of his guards, carrying Winchesters. Sam recognized the guards' surly captain, Steele. Overhead, the clouds had thickened, like wool, turning the sky almost as white as the snow on the ground. There seemed to be no color left in the world.

Frenchy said, "I see he's got his goons—I mean, his guards—with him."

Sam grinned. "Don't let him see me in here," he said, and he wedged himself behind the cabin door.

Karl and Frenchy both had their small-bore shotguns now. Karl put down his pipe and opened the door, and the two miners stepped out, guns ready. Sam watched through the crack where the door met the frame. Cold, damp air came rushing into the cabin.

"Good afternoon, Mr. Hastings," said Karl.

Hastings halted his men. He wore a caped greatcoat, scarf, and a black wide-awake hat. He affected good cheer. "'Afternoon, boys. Mind if we come in? It's a bit cold out here."

He stepped forward but was stopped by Karl's leveled shotgun. At this short distance, even bird shot would do damage. "Vatever you haff to say, you say it from zere."

Hastings's men raised their weapons, but the mine owner motioned them to be calm. Good humor seemingly intact, he spoke to Karl and Frenchy. "That's not very neighborly."

Frenchy said, "Show me a law says we got to be neighborly. You sure ain't been. You been lookin' to jump our claim for a couple months now. We was to let you and your hired guns in the door, you might get what you been after."

Hastings said, "I don't know what you mean by that, but I'll overlook it for now. I've come to do you boys a favor."

"You're leaving Paradise Mountain?" Frenchy cracked.

Hastings made an attempt to smile, but it was plain he didn't appreciate the joke. "I'm giving you a chance to sell your claim."

Indignantly, Karl said, "Ve are not—"

"Let's not beat around the bush," Hastings interrupted, and the mask of good humor disappeared. "Your claim sits right in the middle of a rich vein, the mother lode. You know it and I know it. I also know you can't work the vein by washing gold because it's too deep to reach without machinery. You've got it, but you can't get at it, not the richest part, anyway. I've bought all the other claims along that vein, as far as yours. I'll be tunneling right through Paradise Mountain come spring. Your claim is in my way. For purely logistical reasons I can't go around. If you don't sell, I have to stop my whole operation."

"Sounds good to me," Frenchy said.

Hastings tried to hold his temper. "Well, it doesn't sound good to me. It's unthinkable, after all the money I've invested here, that I would let a broken-down German—"

"Austrian," corrected Karl indignantly.

"—and a nigger stop me. I've got my eye on big things—politics, society—and the gold from Paradise Mountain is going to pay for them. I'm prepared to make you two a more than generous offer. Say, five thousand each?"

Behind Hastings, Steele and the guards fingered their rifles. Their presence added an unspoken threat to Hastings's offer.

"Ve are not interested," Karl told Hastings.

"Why? Everyone else is selling."

"George Pennington did not."

"And George Pennington starved to death. That's just my point. All the gold in the world won't do you any good without food. Two more men died today, from what I hear."

"Haff you gotten zeir claims?"

"I will," Hastings assured him. "So you see, either you sell, or you die. Either way I get your claim. This way you get some money, and, I'll be honest, it's worth it for me to have it all square and legal, in writing. I've heard the rumors about me claim jumping and I don't like them. They hurt, if you must know."

Frenchy said, "Seems to me we die even if we do sell. Don't matter how much money you got, ain't no food up here."

The smile returned to Hastings's lips. "Didn't I mention? I know where there's food to be had."

Both Karl and Frenchy sucked in their breaths.

Hastings went on. "Flour, corn, bacon, sugar—sell, and you'll be able to buy as much as you want."

Karl licked his lips. Scratching his white beard thoughtfully, he glanced inside the cabin door. Sam caught his eye and shook his head, signing him not to go through with the deal.

As Karl turned away from Sam, Hastings said, "You don't have to leave Paradise Mountain, either. You can keep your cabin here, and I'll put you on my payroll come spring. I need strong backs. I even hire Negroes, and there's not many as can say that."

Karl snorted. "No, I do not do zat. I am a prospector. I alvays haff been, I alvays vill be. I vork for myself. I don't go hard-rock mining underground, vis ze cave-ins and explosions—"

"Oh, it's not that bad," scoffed Hastings. "Next season we'll be using that new explosive—dynamite. It's a lot safer than black powder."

"How many dead you had this year?" Frenchy said.

"A few. It's dangerous work, and accidents *do* happen, you know."

"That ain't what I hear," Frenchy said. "I hear it's more'n fifty dead, and plenty more injured."

"You can hear lots of things," Hastings told him. "You can hear the world is flat, if you listen long enough. Now, I'm tired of standing out here in the cold. Are you going to sell or not?"

Karl spoke for both of them. "Ve don't vant you, Mr. Hastings. Ve stay here and ve do not sell. Not now, not ever."

"Bold words, Mr. Eisenreich. I'll have them carved on your tombstone. You boys don't know what you've lost."

"Maybe ve haff enough of food," Karl lied. "Maybe ve stockpiled for ze vinter. I am not a miner for sirty years visout learning somesing, you know."

Hastings didn't know whether to believe the old man or not. His voice took on an edge that had been missing before. "Then maybe you'll die

from something besides starvation." He turned
away, then stopped. "By the way, you boys
haven't seen that bounty hunter Slater, have
you?"

"Slater?" said Karl, with what he hoped
sounded like surprise. "No. Vy?"

"He killed a woman in town last night, then
busted out of jail—with some help. Two men, as
I hear it."

Hastings stared at Karl and Frenchy point-
edly. They stared right back.

Hastings went on. "There's a thousand dollars' reward for Slater's capture. I'm putting up
the money. Whatever our personal differences,
we can't have a killer like that running loose."

"Ve haff not seen him," Karl repeated.

"Well, he might be headed your way. I hear
he did you a good turn the other night, with that
Egan fellow."

Karl shook his head. "Ve haff not seen him."

"Keep your eyes peeled," Hastings said. He
walked off, motioning his guards to join him.
The guards backed up slowly, rifles ready, partly
in case there was trouble, partly to reinforce the
threat of trouble that they themselves represented. Then they turned and followed their boss.

When Hastings and his men were well
upstream, Karl and Frenchy came back in, shivering from the cold. They shut the door, and
Sam stepped from behind it.

"Zere *is* food here," Karl said bitterly. "I knew

it. Damn zat Hastings. He comes here vis his money and his gunmen, and he sinks he can chust take over. And he is doing it, too, by golly."

Sam said, "Where'd he come from, anyway?"

Frenchy said, "Tucson, is what I hear."

Karl and Frenchy looked at Sam. They could not understand why he was suddenly smiling.

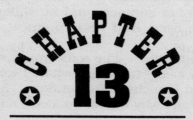

CHAPTER 13

"VY HAFF YOU ZAT SMILE?" KARL ASKED SAM.

Frenchy added, "Either I missed the joke, or you got a strange sense of humor."

"Because it's all clear to me now," Sam told them. He explained the circumstances that had brought him to Paradise Mountain. "Ed Robinette was murdered in Tucson. Hastings told me he'd never been to Tucson. There's only one reason he'd lie about that. If he didn't kill Robinette himself, he ordered it done. That's why he's been after me—he was afraid I'd find out. Do you know anything more about him, like where he got his money?"

Frenchy shook his head. "Not much. He camped up here for a while in the early summer.

Claimed to be a sourdough, like the rest of us, but I never seen him wash out a pan of dirt. Seemed like he was checking out the area more than anything else."

"*Ja,*" said Karl, "and he spent a lot of time at ze assayer's office, I remember zat now."

Frenchy said, "Anyways, he left for a while, then he come back with all his equipment and money."

"And his gunmen," Karl added.

Sam paced around the little cabin. If Harry Hastings was behind Robinette's death, he was behind Laramie's death as well. It took an effort for Sam not to go charging out the door after Hastings and his men. But he couldn't. The guards would shoot him before he got within fifty feet of Hastings. He would have to get his revenge later.

He thought of something else. Even though he now knew who had ordered Robinette to be killed, he was going to need proof before he could collect that reward.

"It's time for me to pay another visit to the Hastings Mining Company," he said. "Do you boys have a spare gun?"

Karl pushed his squirrel gun toward Sam. "Take zis, if you like."

"No, you might need that yourself. How 'bout a pistol— either of you got one?"

"Vait," said Karl, remembering, "I do haff a pistol." He went to the corner, rummaged in his pack, and pulled out an oilcloth-wrapped bundle. "I bought zis on ze Stanislaus River, in forty-nine. I haff never used it, zough."

He opened the bundle, revealing a monstrous old .44-caliber Colt Dragoon. "Here."

Sam took the weapon. It weighed four and a half pounds and, when fired, would have the kick of an ornery mule. After years of neglect it was rusted through. Sam couldn't even thumb back the hammer. Still, it could be cleaned and put back in working condition.

"How about ammunition?" Sam asked.

From the pack Karl produced an old powder flask and pouches filled with lead balls and percussion caps.

Sam regarded the ammunition dubiously. "How old is this?"

"I am not certain," Karl admitted, sheepishly.

"Think it's any good?" Frenchy asked Sam.

"I hope I won't have to find out," Sam replied. Then he grew more serious. "I think you boys are in danger here. Hastings will do anything to get your claim. You might want to consider pulling out and going back to town, or holing up with some friends."

"And leave our claim vacant for Hastings to steal?" Karl exclaimed. "Never. So vat if ve cannot vork ze richest part. Ve are doing all right on ze part ve can vork. Ven zat is panned out, maybe zen ve vill sell. Not before. I don't clear out of here for no vun."

Sam looked at Frenchy. The black man nodded agreement with his partner.

"It's your call," Sam told them. "But be careful whenever you leave the cabin."

Sam spent the rest of the afternoon working on the pistol. With difficulty he broke it down, cleaned it, and oiled it. He loaded it, using cutout pieces of felt to wad the powder and balls, then he placed percussion caps on the cylinder nipples.

"You want to go out and test it?" Frenchy said.

Sam shook his head. "Can't take the chance. I'm afraid Hastings is having this cabin watched, in case I show up here."

The gray day faded into night. The wind picked up, whistling mournfully around the miners' cabin. Inside, it was chilly, even with the roaring fire. Karl had gone out hunting, but he found no game. "Zere is no animal stupid enough to be out in zis weather, by golly," he pronounced upon his return. "I found footprints up ze hill, zough. Fresh made, zey vere."

"Hastings's men," said Sam. "The cabin *is* being watched."

The miners' supper was one small flapjack each, with coffee. Again, Sam refused to share their food.

"You got to eat something," Frenchy told him. "You going to starve up, if you don't."

"I'll be all right," Sam assured him.

At last it was dark. The two miners had no cooking grease left, but they did have a can of axle grease that they used on their rocker and some of their other tools. Sam smeared some on his battered face, to protect the exposed flesh from the cold. Before leaving, he borrowed some sulfur matches from Karl. "How far to Hastings's mine?" he asked.

Frenchy answered. "It's over the rise and east a mile or so, but you'd have to be part Injun to find your way there in the dark, in this weather."

Sam smiled faintly. "I guess you would."

Sam stuck the big Colt Dragoon in his waistband and buttoned what was left of his coat around him. "I should be back about daybreak," he told Karl and Frenchy. He listened to the wailing wind, and he added, "If there is any daybreak."

He pushed open the cabin door, which resisted because of the wind pressure against it, and then he was gone.

CHAPTER 14

THE FIRST TIME SAM HAD VISITED THE Hastings Mining Company, he had intended to be seen. This time was different.

The bitter wind sliced through his clothing like a knife through butter. It swirled at his back and shoulders as he struggled up the snow-covered hill. It froze the sweat on his chest and back. He didn't worry about encountering any of Hastings's guards near the cabin now. Hastings would have withdrawn them for the night—no sense having them freeze to death. Tomorrow they would return.

The intense cold had frozen the snow, so that Sam had to thrust his feet through a hard crust of it with each step, then pull them out again. He'd thought about making snowshoes, but he'd decided that the ground was too rough. In a way the snow was a blessing, though, because its luminescence gave him some idea where he was going.

He crested Paradise Mountain, then turned east. On this side of the mountain the horizon opened dramatically, because nothing remained of the forest but tree stumps. The voracious appetite of Hastings's mill had extended this far. Next year, who knew how much more of the mountain it would devour? Sam's path was broken by ice-choked gullies and ravines, and he had to be wary of his footing. Laboriously, he made his way down the ravines, then up the far sides, his numbed hands and feet slipping on the icy rock, the wind shrieking in his ears. He was tired. He wanted to lie down and sleep. He felt a pleasant warmth spreading over him, like a blanket. He knew that if he just slept here for a little while, he'd be refreshed and able to . . .

He shook his head violently and got to his feet. Without realizing it, he had sat down. Another few minutes and he would have frozen to death. He flapped his arms and stuffed snow into his eyes, trying to shock himself awake. He started walking again, stumbling along.

Then, in the distance, he saw the glow of lights. It was the Hastings mine.

As he approached the complex he moved slowly, watchfully. Even in this weather Hastings might have guards out. Hastings hadn't gotten as far as he had by taking chances. Ahead of Sam, the great processing mill was a malignant shadow against the snowy mountainside, but lights shone from the guards' barracks and cookhouse. The shadows of people were visible through the unshuttered windows of Hastings's two-story house. The mine owner and his "lady" friend must be entertaining. A group of men came onto the gallery, apparently to clear their heads of the stuffy air inside. Sam thought he recognized Marshal Tom Jeffcoat among them.

"Surprise, surprise," he muttered to himself.

The figures on the gallery went back inside. Sam waited in the freezing cold, jaws clenched tight so that his teeth wouldn't chatter. When things in Hastings's house quieted down, he sneaked along to the company office. There was no one inside, not at this time of night. The front door was unlocked. Sam opened it and slipped in.

Sam drew the shutters. He found a kerosene lantern and lit it. Anyone might see the light, but he'd have to take that chance. If he was lucky, they would think it was Hastings's clerk, working late. Quickly, Sam searched around. He wasn't sure what he was looking for. The place was a jumble of desks, piled with ledgers and receipts, with blueprints and payroll sheets and with correspondence.

In one corner was a large safe. Sam tried the lever, but it was locked, and he was no safe-cracker. No matter, he thought. The safe was where operating funds and payrolls would be kept. Hastings's foreman and probably his chief clerk would have the combination. The mine owner would not hide anything incriminating to himself in there, in case one of the others should find it. The room's largest desk must belong to Hastings. Sam sat in the chair and opened the drawers, rifling through the papers. Through the building's thin walls, he heard a burst of laughter from the house. The lower right-hand drawer was locked. With his sheath knife Sam pried it open. Inside was a steel box. It, too, was locked. Sam worked at the lock with his knife. He strained, prying it, and the lock broke with a loud *thwang*.

Sam waited, to see if anyone had heard. There was no sound but the wailing wind and more laughter from next door. Sam sat on the floor, shielding the lantern with his coat. The steel box contained more papers—correspondence with lawyers and politicians, along with assayers' reports valuing samples of ore at anywhere from two to three thousand dollars a ton. There was also a sketch of Paradise Mountain, showing the rough course of the mother lode. Miners' claims had been marked off along the lode, with a red "X" in the corners of those now in Hastings's possession. Sam recognized the next claim in line for takeover as Karl and Frenchy's. After the sketch came the deeds to the claims, bound with a red ribbon. The deeds were handwritten, witnessed by Hastings's clerk. Over half of the claims had been purchased from William MacDonald, William Ford, and . . . John J. Egan.

Sam smiled grimly to himself. He hadn't realized that Egan and his friends were such expert prospectors.

The last document was more formal. As Sam read it, his jaw set. It established a partnership between Edward A. Robinette, of Tucson, and Henry Hastings, of the same city. Under terms of the agreement, Robinette lent Hastings seventy-five thousand dollars to establish a mining company. In return for capitalization of the company, Robinette was to receive sixty percent of the net profits. Hastings would receive the other forty percent of the profits plus a director's salary. It seemed a fair agreement.

Sam stuffed the agreement in his shirt and blew out the lantern. Hastings had arranged Robinette's murder out of pure greed. He must have come to Robinette with the ore assays from Paradise Mountain and his idea for the mine. Robinette had agreed to lend the money, under a secret partnership, for a percentage of the profits. Once the operation was under way—perhaps even before—Hastings had decided he didn't want to share the profits. He wanted them all for himself, just as he wanted all of Paradise Mountain for himself. He'd had Robinette killed and this agreement stolen. The crime had been carefully staged to look like a robbery, but this document had been the sole object of the theft.

And who had killed Robinette? The same man who had killed Laramie. Only he had not used a metal poker to kill the girl. That had been another plant. He had used a sawed-off baseball bat.

Johnny Egan.

Marshal Jeffcoat and Tracy had lied about Egan being in Paradise Mountain when Robinette's murder had occurred. No matter how many witnesses they could produce to Egan's presence, it didn't matter. They would all be on Hastings's payroll.

Sam wondered if this partnership agreement was enough to get him the extra thousand dollars of the reward. Hastings and Egan had probably thrown the rest of Robinette's papers away. They would have been of no use to them.

Sam left the office. Tomorrow, Hastings would know the office had been broken into. He would probably guess who had done it, but it wouldn't make any difference. The mine owner was looking for Sam anyway. This would just give him extra incentive.

Wraithlike, Sam flitted between the buildings. There was one more place he wanted to visit while he was here. He ascended the hill alongside the stamping mill, making for the strange excavation up top.

He climbed as rapidly as he could, following the track that branched off to the excavation. The excavation wasn't the entrance to a mine shaft; Sam could tell that. There was a large tarp across the front, protecting—and hiding—whatever was inside. Sam took a last look around. He was alone. He pulled the tarp aside and went in.

After the bright snow backdrop outside, the darkness in the excavation was total. Sam stood for a second, letting himself become acclimated. He seemed to be in a medium-sized room. He smelled dampness and wood, and something else that he couldn't believe. Food. He put out his hands and touched a wooden crate. There were more crates alongside it.

Should he light a match? He had to take the chance. He pulled out one of Karl's sulfur matches and struck it on the side of the crate. He held the match aloft in wonderment.

He was in a large room, carved out of the mountain's living rock. From top to bottom the room was packed with food. There were hogsheads of bacon, sacks of flour, corn, and potatoes, barrels of sugar and salt.

The match burned down. Sam shook it out and lit another, wandering deeper into the cave. The hijacked freight shipments—this was where they had all gone. Hastings's men had stolen them. Hastings was starving out the placer miners so that he could buy their claims, then he would get his money back by selling them food at inflated prices. And when they were broke, he would force them to come work for him.

He didn't miss a trick, Sam thought.

Sam's hunger, combined with the sight of so much food, got the best of him. Shaking out the second match, he sliced open a sack of potatoes, took one out, and ate it raw. He thought of all the men sick with scurvy, and of how these potatoes could have prevented that disease. He stuffed his coat pockets with more of the potatoes, then he prepared to leave. As he started out he heard voices.

"The boss said he saw a light up here. I told him it was nothing."

"Better check anyway. You know how he is."

The tarp was swung wide and three men entered, with a lantern. There was nowhere for Sam to hide. He was caught in the lantern's glare. The speaker was Willie—or William MacDonald—with his Scots cap. With him were one of the guards, and Johnny Egan, carrying his baseball bat.

The newcomers jumped back, startled. "Slater," snarled Egan. He lifted his bat while Willie and the guard drew their pistols.

Sam dived into Egan, who fell into the other two, knocking them down and putting out the lantern. Before Egan and the others could recover, Sam was out the cave entrance. Gunshots sounded behind him. He heard curses and men fumbling at the tarp.

Sam started down the hill, but the shots had attracted more of Hastings's guards. He heard cries from below and saw the guards coming on, outlined against the snow.

He looked back. Egan and the others had emerged from the cave. They were firing at him. Crouched low, Sam ran along the hillside, then upward. Egan and the others pursued him.

Sam kept climbing. It was the only direction open to him. If all the trees had not been cut down, he would have had cover. As it was, he was plainly visible against the snow. More shots sounded. Bullets zipped by. Others kicked up little gouts of snow, or thunked into pine stumps.

"Spread out," Egan called. "Don't let him get away."

Sam drew the Colt Dragoon from his waistband. His pursuers were close now. He was tired and weak. He had to slow them down, or it was all over for him. He turned. A shadowy form loomed out of the dark. Sam thumbed back the pistol's hammer. As he did, the mainspring broke, from rust and cold. In front of him the man chuckled and raised his own weapon. Desperate, Sam picked up a rock. He pointed the pistol and hit the tip of the hammer with the rock. The pistol fired with a loud bang and a flash; Sam felt the recoil from his wrist to his shoulder. The man in front of Sam gurgled, staggered, and dropped to the snow. The shot made the rest of Hastings's men hold back. They redoubled their fire on Sam, muzzle flashes winking on the snowy hillside. That gave Sam the breather he needed. He turned and kept going.

He reached the mountaintop and found himself on a flat ledge. He took a step off the far side, and his foot met nothing but air. He recovered his balance and stepped back. The ledge ended in a sheer drop. He couldn't see how far the drop went. He turned right, but Hastings's men had already blocked the mountaintop in that direction. He started left, but he was cut off in that direction as well. More guards were coming at him from downhill.

He heard Johnny Egan laughing. "We've got you now, Slater," he called.

Hastings's men came on slowly now, in a line, holding their fire.

Sam squinted over the ledge, but he could not see the bottom. For all he knew, the drop could be a thousand feet. He had no choice, though.

Stuffing the pistol back in his waistband, Sam lowered himself off the ledge until he was dangling in the air, hanging on by his hands. Then, as the sound of footsteps came closer, he let go.

CHAPTER 15

AS SAM FELL, HE SWUNG HIMSELF INWARD, toward the face of the rock wall. He hit the rock and slid down it in freefall, tearing himself to pieces. He scrabbled for handholds and footholds, smashing his fingers, ripping apart his gloves and the toes of his boots. The heavy pistol in his waistband gouged his stomach. He began picking up speed. He figured he was dead.

Then his feet hit something with a teeth-rattling jar. He bent to absorb the blow, overbalanced on the icy surface, and almost toppled over backward. He threw himself forward and hugged the rock.

He was on a narrow ledge. He stood there,

trembling with fright and pain, dazed and bleeding and trying to catch his breath. He shivered as the frigid wind cut through what was left of his clothes.

Far above him he heard voices, shredded by the wind:

"Christ, he jumped."

"It's better'n what he'd have got from us." That voice belonged to Johnny Egan.

"Still, it took nerve to do it," said the first man.

"Do you see him?" asked a third voice.

"I don't see nothing," replied the first speaker.

"I don't want to see nothing," said yet another voice, that Sam recognized as Willie's. "I'm scared to get near the edge."

Egan said, "Let's get out of here. I'm freezing. Wait till the boss hears about this."

A little shower of pebbles rained down past Sam as the men turned and left.

Sam would have liked to stay on the ledge until daylight, when he could see what he was doing, but that was impossible. Either he would freeze to death by then, or he'd fall asleep and plunge into the void. He closed his eyes for a minute, to stop his head from spinning.

He had to get down the mountain. In the dark there was no way to tell how high up he was, or how far this ledge extended.

He felt backward with his right foot. Immediately the foot was in the air. The ledge seemed to be about a yard wide, and that was being generous. The drop on the other side could be two feet or two hundred. There was no way to tell.

Which way to go? One was as good as the other, Sam decided. He began working to his right, feeling with his foot and hand, sliding along, being careful on the icy surface. The ledge narrowed, then ended. Sam looked over his shoulder, but he saw only blackness.

He felt across and down with his foot, found a projection, got his hand on a hold to match it. Carefully he lowered himself down, bringing his left foot and hand down to the places formerly occupied by the others. Even in the cold wind, sweat was running down his back. His hands and feet felt like blocks of wood, and the blood had frozen on them, making them slippery in addition. He worked his way to a fissure in the rock, inched down it to another ledge. He moved along the ledge but after a few yards, it ended. Sam stepped out, feeling for a foothold. He found one, on an uneven rock. He reached with his hand. He searched up and down in the darkness, but could find nothing. He blinked sweat out of his eyes. He tried again with his hand. Still he found nothing. The rock wall was smooth. He was at an awkward angle; he couldn't go back. He would have to push himself across the rock and grab with his hand, hoping to find something to hold on to.

He took a breath, then pushed out, swinging

his hand out as far as he could. His fingers found a small projection. They dug into its cracks, straining for a hold. As they did, his foot slipped on the ice. He tried to recover, but his foot fell off its hold. He grabbed frantically at the rocks with his hands, but there was nothing to hold on to, and he was falling. He bounced off something hard, then he was in the air, turning slowly. He fell down the mountainside, bouncing head over heels, twisting sideways, being smashed to pieces. Everything was spinning. He couldn't get control of himself. Then there were bright stars in front of his eyes, flashing pain, and he was still falling. . . .

Harry Hastings stood on the long gallery of his house, flanked by Marshal Tom Jeffcoat and Steve Tracy, owner of the Metropolitan Saloon. Jeffcoat and Tracy each held one of their host's excellent cigars. The three men had been staring up at the mountainside above the stamping mill, watching the gunshots and the chase of the unknown intruder. Then the shots had stopped. The trio stood, shivering in the night air, wondering what had happened.

They saw shadows against the snow as Egan and his men came back down the mountain. Egan carried his baseball bat. The returning men were in high spirits.

"You were right, boss," Egan cried as he

came up. "There *was* somebody in the cave. And guess who it was? Slater!"

The group on the gallery stirred. "Slater!" said Hastings.

"Are you sure?" Jeffcoat said.

Egan swaggered up onto the gallery. "I'm sure. I was as close to him as I am to you."

"Where is he now?" Hastings said.

"We chased him up the mountain, and he jumped off the cliff, to get away from us."

"Is he dead?"

"He must be. That's a hell of a drop there. Nobody could have lived through it. We'll go and bring in his body tomorrow."

Hastings turned to his guests with a big smile. "Gentlemen, I believe this calls for a drink. But first—Mr. Steele, drinks for your guards, at my expense. Tell them to take the rest of the night off as a reward."

The usually surly Steele grinned. "Right, Mr. Hastings."

"Let's go back inside, where it's warm," Hastings told his guests. To Egan he said, "Good work, Johnny."

"Thanks, Mr. Hastings." Egan swung the bat over his shoulder cockily.

The men went inside. Egan went with them. As Hastings's chief enforcer, he felt himself allowed the privileges of the house. Some of the other guests might not have liked that, but they were afraid to say it out loud.

Hastings's girlfriend was waiting inside. It had been too cold for her to be out on the gallery, and anyway, she hadn't much cared what was happening up the mountainside.

"Drinks for everybody, Rose," Hastings told her.

The girl complied, pouring bonded bourbon and passing it around. She had a hard, angular face and a good body. There were dark circles under her eyes. They called her the Yellow Rose, because of her corn-silk hair, which was set off tonight by a red satin dress. She handed Egan his glass a bit fearfully, at arm's length. She knew Egan's reputation with women, and she thanked God she was under Hastings's protection, where she didn't have to worry about men like that. Such a luxury wouldn't last, of course—Hastings would eventually tire of her—but it was nice while it lasted.

Hastings himself didn't drink, just as he did not smoke, but he liked to cater to what he saw as his guests' weaknesses. It helped ensure their loyalty. Also, he felt that men who were attracted to liquor often had wills that might more easily be bent than those who were not.

Hastings raised his voice. "A toast, gentlemen. To good fortune." The other men—and Rose, who needed no excuse—raised their glasses and drank. Hastings went on, congratulating himself. "Here we were, just discussing the need for eliminating Slater, and now, it seems, Mr. Slater has eliminated himself. That should make you particularly happy, Mr. Jeffcoat, as the man who let him escape."

"It wasn't my fault," growled the marshal. "How was I supposed to know somebody was going to blow up the jail?"

"Speaking of which," said Steve Tracy. "We still don't know who did it."

"I have an idea who it was," Hastings said, "but it's of no consequence. They shall be dealt with, but Slater was the one that counted. He's the only man who could have stopped us. Now that he's dead, nothing stands in our way."

"You mean in 'your' way, don't you?" said Tracy.

"Come, come, Mr. Tracy. You don't still harbor ill feelings over our lovely Rose, I hope?"

Tracy said nothing. His glum look was answer enough. He had been able to fulfill his sexual needs with his other girls, but Rose had been his star. She had been more than that to him as well. She had been something he was afraid to admit to himself. When Hastings had taken her, it was like Tracy had been emasculated. There was nothing he could do, however. Hastings's money called the turn in Paradise Mountain. If it wasn't for the mine owner, Tracy wouldn't be mayor.

Hastings went on, consoling his rival in love. "We all share in the profits of this enterprise, gentlemen. As my mine grows I hire more workers. Which means that your saloon and girls bring in more money, Steve. And it means more fines for you to collect, Jeffcoat—when you're not fleecing the innocents at the tables."

Jeffcoat squirmed. Cards were an obsession for him, they always had been. He couldn't help it.

Egan said, "What about me, boss?"

Hastings smiled. "We can always find work for you, Johnny."

That was true. Hastings had to find work for Egan, because Egan was likely to become trouble, otherwise. The mine owner was glad to have him on his side, but he was also a bit scared of him. Egan's penchant for violence could erupt at any time, against anyone. Some men—Hastings was one of them—killed for business. Egan killed because he enjoyed it. He enjoyed crushing skulls with that damned bat, watching eyes pop out of their sockets.

Hastings didn't know much about Egan. The man claimed to have been a member of the notorious Tenth Avenue Gang, in New York. He said he had killed his first man when he was fourteen. He had used a baseball bat for the job, and he'd liked it so much, it had become his trademark. He'd joined the army during the war and had served with distinction, but upon his discharge he had resumed his old ways. He'd created so much havoc that he'd gotten in trouble with Tammany Hall, the Tenth Avenue Gang's patron, and had been forced to come west. Hastings had met him in Paradise Mountain and immediately put him to work.

Hastings went on. "Your next job will be to get rid of that German and his nigger partner."

"Maybe we should just let them starve to death," suggested Tracy. The saloon keeper never ran from a fight, but he wasn't much on violence for its own sake. "It's the easiest way, and it's inevitable."

"Or they could starve the other way," said Egan hopefully, "the way Pennington did. While we held a gun to his head." He laughed.

"No," said Hastings. "I'm tired of beating around the bush with those two. I'm tired of waiting to get that claim. It's best if they just disappear. We can always say they sold out and tried to make their way back down the mountain. No one will ever know what happened to them. No one will care, really. Men like that are quickly forgotten."

"When do we take them out?" Egan asked.

"Tomorrow. Meanwhile—Rose, pour our guests more drinks. We have some celebrating to do. Tomorrow, I expect we'll have even more."

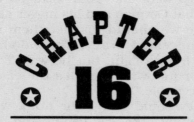

CHAPTER 16

COLD. COLD WAS ALL THAT SAM KNEW, IN every bone, in every pore of his body.

He seemed to be in some sort of cold, soft cocoon. For a moment he wondered if he was dead, then he realized that he must have landed in a snowdrift in his fall off the mountain. The thick snow had no doubt saved his life.

He opened his eyes but saw nothing. He could not tell if he was upside down or right side up. It was as if he were in suspended animation.

Starting at his extremities, he began working his body parts to see how many were broken. At the end of his self-examination, everything seemed to be intact. He considered this a miracle, because his body felt as smashed up as a bag of sawdust. Only the numbing effect of the snow kept the pain from being unbearable.

Something sharp was stabbing his gut. He moved his hand and touched the hammer of Karl Eisenreich's Colt Dragoon in his waistband. He shifted the weapon, then he rocked back and forth in the snowdrift, grimacing as waves of pain rolled over him. He determined that he was upside down. Awkwardly, he pushed with his feet and hands until he emerged from the deep snow.

It was past dawn. The sky was gray and forbidding, with the promise of more snow. Once out of the drift's protective cover, he felt the bitter wind blow over him, and he knew that he had to get moving. The snow had been cold, but it had provided enough insulation to keep him from freezing to death while he was unconscious.

He lay there a minute, resting, regaining his strength. With an effort, ignoring the gut-wrenching pain, he pushed himself to his knees, then to his feet. He stumbled and regained his balance, like a drunken man.

He was about halfway down the slope of the mountain. Because of the low clouds, he couldn't see the spot from where he'd jumped last night. The inside of the snowdrift where he'd lain was stained pink from his blood. His clothes were in tatters.

He had to get to Karl and Frenchy's cabin. Then he heard noises, coming down the mountainside. There were voices as well. They could only belong to Hastings's men, come to see if he was dead.

On his stomach, so that he wouldn't leave tracks, Sam shimmied across the crusted snow to a nearby boulder. He shuddered as he realized that if he had landed just a few yards over, he would have hit that boulder and been smashed to an unrecognizable pulp. He reached the huge rock. Gasping with pain, he climbed it and peered over the rim.

Willie MacDonald and one of Hastings's gunmen known as Missouri Jack came down the mountain, half sliding, half walking in the deep snow. Huddled in their heavy coats, they searched the tree-and-rock-covered expanse of the mountainside.

"See him yet?" asked Jack.

"No," said Willie, teeth chattering, from the depths of his buffalo-robe coat. Willie hated the cold. He'd come to the southwest to get away from winter weather, and here he found himself colder than ever. It wasn't fair.

"He fell a long way," Jack observed. Jack was a dull-witted fellow with a notch missing from one ear, courtesy of an old barroom fight. Working for Hastings was the closest he had ever come to a regular job. "You sure we ain't got to bury him?" he asked Willie for what must have been the dozenth time.

"No," Willie replied, exasperated. Once again

he explained. "We just have to make sure he's dead, is all, so's the boss can spread the news that a dangerous whore killer like Slater is out of the way. The coyotes and crows can have the body. What the hell, they get hungry, too, you know."

"Hey, lookit!" said Jack, pointing. "Over there! Is that him?"

Willie followed the Missourian's finger to where something lay crumpled in a snowdrift. "Yeah," he said. "I think it is."

Both men unbuttoned their coats and drew their pistols. They advanced on the snowdrift and stood over the battered form, which lay facedown in the drift, inert.

"Is he dead?" Jack wondered.

"He must be," Willie said. "Look at all that blood."

"Let's just see here," Jack said. With the toe of his boot, he turned the body over.

As he did, Sam sprang from the snow, knife drawn. With one hand he plunged the knife into Jack's chest. With the other hand he knocked Willie's pistol aside.

Willie was too surprised to react. It was as if a ghost had attacked him. Sam threw Willie to the ground, choking him. Willie struggled under the powerful hands of this tattered, bleeding apparition while Jack breathed his last nearby.

Sam slowly squeezed the life out of Willie. He looked at the gunman's face, and all he could see was Laramie and what they had done to her, and that vision made him squeeze harder. Beneath him, Willie's legs thrashed wildly, his tongue protruded from his mouth, and his eyes bulged out of their sockets. His face turned blue. The thrashing of the legs gradually lessened, then stopped. He gave a shudder, and was still.

Sam kept his grip on the dead man's throat for a moment, to make sure. Then he stood. He was breathing heavily, his thirst for revenge not abated—but whetted.

He took Willie's plaid Scots cap from the snow, brushed it off, and put it on. He was glad to have something warm on his head again. He took the dead man's heavy buffalo-robe coat and put that on, too, in place of of his own, which had become a collection of holes and slashes bound together by a small bit of cloth. Willie's coat was small on Sam's big frame, but it would have to do. Sam took the stolen potatoes from his old coat pockets and stuck them in the new one. His bloodied toes stuck out of his torn boots, but neither of the dead men wore anything like the same size, so he cut strips off their wool shirts and wrapped them around his feet for protection. He searched both men for food, but found none.

He took the dead men's pistols and stuck them in the coat's deep pockets. Then he started off to Karl and Frenchy's cabin, sucking snow to slake his thirst.

The easiest way to the cabin would be along the stream, but an Apache never approached anything by the most direct route. An Apache circled around, studying his destination, learning if it was safe to go near it first. So Sam worked his way along the rough mountainside, staying in the cover of the trees. It was hard on him. Several times he nearly passed out from exhaustion and pain and hunger.

As he finally neared the cabin he found a vantage point above it and halted. He squatted, watching. The cold wind cut to his bones, but he forced himself to ignore it.

Smoke curled from the cabin's stone chimney, to be torn away by the wind. Carefully, Sam searched the broken hillside between himself and the cabin. Beneath the snow-laden boughs of some pines, he saw movement. There—to the right—was more. Armed men were hidden all around the cabin. Sam recognized the bearded, hulking form of Johnny Egan among them. Egan and his men were slowly advancing from three sides. They must be trying to get close, then rush the cabin, hoping to overwhelm the surprised occupants before they could fight back. Gunfire would alert the other miners along the stream, who would come to investigate; and if they did that, whatever lie that Hastings had concocted about the fates of Karl and Frenchy couldn't be told.

Sam tipped the Scots cap low over his eyes. He stood and started down the hill, hands deep in his coat pockets.He looked too tall to be Willie, but he hoped that Egan and his men wouldn't notice the difference until it was too late.

He was in plain view now. One of Egan's men saw him. The man nudged another. Frantically, the two of them motioned Sam to get under cover.

At that moment the cabin door opened and Karl emerged, with his squirrel gun and hunting bag. He took a step then saw a man in a Scots cap coming down the hill. Quickly he dodged back into the cabin. In the brittle air Sam heard the sound of the door slamming.

There were moans from Egan's hidden gang of claim jumpers. As Sam drew near, the closest one stood. "Willie, what the hell's the matter with—" He stopped, eyes wide. "You ain't Willie. Christ, it's—"

Sam pulled the pistols from his coat pockets and began firing. The man nearest to him took a bullet in the chest and dropped with a surprised look on his face. Sam turned and shot the second man, who spun, staggered, and fell, clutching his ribs.

Sam dived for cover behind the pine trees as the rest of Egan's men opened up on him. He stuffed the pistols back in his coat pockets and crawled over to the dead claim jumper. He took the man's Winchester and his ammunition, then crawled back to his vantage point in the trees. Bullets buried themselves in the snow around him; they knocked caked snow from the pine boughs overhead.

Sam returned the fire slowly, aiming at the muzzle flashes among the pines and rocks.

Behind him, the wounded man moved in agony, near death. Sam used his ammunition sparingly. If he ran out, he was dead. From the cabin, Karl and Frenchy's squirrel guns opened up. The gunfire boomed among the snowy mountain peaks and down the valley.

Sam ducked his head as the bullets began buzzing more thickly around him. He backed into a new position behind a snowbank. Egan and his men ignored the harmless fire from the cabin and concentrated on him. They were working their way around him, closing in on three sides. Sam aimed and fired at a dark figure outlined against the snow. The figure dropped to the earth, but Sam couldn't tell if he had been hit or not.

A bullet whined at Sam from behind. Egan's men had surrounded him. The level of gunfire intensified. Sam buried himself in the snowbank, throwing up a breastwork of snow to protect his rear. There were so many bullets flying at him that he couldn't raise up to chance a return shot.

Suddenly a voice cried, "There's men coming, from upstream. A bunch of them."

Over the gunfire Johnny Egan could be heard swearing. Then he shouted. "Come on, boys. Let's get out of here."

The firing slackened, then stopped. There was the sound of retreating footsteps in the crusty snow. When the claim jumpers were gone, Sam got up cautiously. The claim jumpers had left behind the two men that Sam had killed. He had seen these two around town. They weren't mine guards; they were unemployed toughs, men with nothing to link them to Hastings—nothing that anyone knew about.

Sam started toward the cabin, still carrying the dead man's Winchester.

"That's far enough, Willie," cried Frenchy's voice from inside the cabin.

Too tired to answer, Sam removed the plaid Scots cap, revealing his long, straw-colored hair.

"Sam!" he heard Frenchy exclaim.

The cabin door opened, and Frenchy came out, followed by Karl with his hobbling arthritic gait. "Sam!" Karl cried.

The two prospectors came up to Sam, taking in his battered condition. "Damn," Frenchy said, "every time I see you, you look worse. You took up wildcat fightin' or somethin'?"

"I been jumping off mountains," Sam told him. "It's a hell of a sport." He pulled Karl's Colt Dragoon from his waistband and returned it to the old Austrian. "Thanks for the loan."

"Did she vork?" Karl said.

"One fella thought so."

Frenchy said, "Did you find anything at Hastings's?"

"Plenty," Sam told him. "More than I—"

There was shouting from upstream, as a large group of armed miners approached. "Christ," one of them yelled. "There's Sam Slater! Somebody get a rope!"

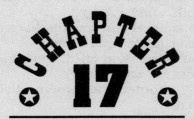

CHAPTER 17

THE CROWD OF MINERS RUSHED UP ANGRI-
ly. They were bearded and emaciated, and they
carried a variety of rifles, shotguns, and pistols.
In their excitement, they forgot what had
brought them here as they grabbed hold of Sam.
Karl and Frenchy tried to reason with them, but
they wouldn't listen, pushing the two prospectors aside.

"Come on," they cried. "String him up."

"Son of a bitch kilt Laramie. He ain't gettin'
away with that."

"You heard what Mr. Hastings said. There's a
thousand dollars' reward for him—dead or alive."

They manhandled Sam to the nearest tree.

Sam tried to speak, but somebody slugged him in the mouth, and he sagged.

Then a squirrel gun was discharged into the air. Everyone quieted and turned.

"Vil you *listen*!" Karl cried, stamping his foot. "Sam did not kill zat voman."

"Yeah?" shouted the miners, disbelieving. "Then who did?"

"Johnny Egan did it," Sam told them. "On the orders of Harry Hastings."

"Hastings?" the miners said. "Why would Hastings want Laramie killed?"

Sam wrenched away from the men who were holding him. "So that I'd be blamed for it. So that you men would do what you were trying to do just now—hang me, and get me out of Hastings's way."

"What's Hastings got against you, Slater?"

"He had a man murdered in Tucson. I came here to find the man's killer. Turns out Egan killed the fellow, on Hastings's order—just like he did Laramie. Think about it. Am I right, or was Egan one of the leaders of the lynch mob, back in town, whipping you boys up to hang me?"

The miners looked at each other. "I recollect he was, at that," said a scurvy-racked youngster, whose condition made him look twice his age.

Sam went on. "Hastings borrowed money from this man in Tucson. Rather than pay him back, he had him killed."

He tapped his coat. "I've got documents in here to prove it. They also prove that Hastings is behind all the claim jumping that's been going on around here."

As the miners muttered among themselves, Sam went on. "That's what the shooting was about just now. Karl and Frenchy here got attacked by claim jumpers. And who do you think was leading the claim jumpers? Johnny Egan, that's who. They were going to kill Karl and Frenchy, steal their claim, then 'sell' it to Hastings. That's how Hastings has been getting all his claims—the ones he can't persuade you boys to turn over to him. I've seen the deeds. If you believe those deeds, you'll believe Johnny Egan is the greatest prospector in the west."

The miners looked at each other uneasily, anger mounting.

"But that's not all," Sam told them. "I know where there's food."

That statement really got their attention. "It's at Hastings's mine," Sam said. "In a cave near the top of the mountain. There's more food there than you men could eat in *two* winters—a ton of it, at least. All those hijacked shipments—that's where they've gone."

The men grew angrier still, cursing and pawing the ground with their feet, like bulls.

"That's right," Sam shouted above the noise. "While you've been here starving, all the food you could ever want has been right under your noses. I've seen it myself. And here's proof." He pulled the potatoes from his coat pockets and began tossing them to the crowd. The black-gummed miners scrambled for them, the lucky ones who came up with them munching them raw. Other men tore them from their hands, taking bites for themselves, their diseased gums leaving blood on the potato skins.

"Take it easy," Sam told the miners, "there's plenty for everybody, at Hastings's mine."

He tossed the last two potatoes to Karl and Frenchy, who ate like the rest. "After Hastings got your claims, he was going to get his money back by selling this food to you at inflated prices. Then, when you were broke, he was going to make you work for him."

"The bastard!" men yelled.

Someone cried, "I say we go to the mine and get us some of that food!"

"What if Hastings won't give it to us?" another miner said.

"Then we take it!"

That statement brought a roar of approval.

A few of the men weren't so sure. "Hastings has got all those men, all those guns."

"You'll never have a better chance," Sam told them. "In a few days most of you will be so weak from hunger you won't be able to stand, much less fight. Then you'll have to do anything Hastings wants you to do."

"Are you coming with us, Slater?" cried one of the miners.

Sam let out his breath. Two days earlier many of these same men had tried to beat him to death. A few minutes ago they had been ready to string him up. Now they wanted him on their side. "Yeah. I'm coming." He turned. "Karl, Frenchy—are you in?"

Karl was so excited he was almost hopping up and down. "You are right, by golly. I go vis you."

Frenchy nodded calmly. "Me, too."

"On to Hastings's mine!" shouted the men, intoxicated with the prospect of food.

"Wait!" said Sam. "Only a small portion of the Paradise Mountain miners are here. Send your best runner back to town, another around the claims. Have them get everybody they can up to Hastings's mine. Hastings has a lot of men and a lot of ammunition. We'll keep them busy till the rest of you get there."

"Pete! Chris!" said Frenchy, singling out the two fastest runners.

As the two young men started back for town, there was a chorus of yells from the remaining miners. "All right, boys. Let's go!"

"You'd better take a back trail up to the mine," Sam warned. "Hastings is no fool. He knows I got away. He knows I found out what he's been up to. He'll have guards out."

But the miners no longer listened. Even

while Sam was still talking, they started down-stream toward the main road, half running, half walking, jostling to get nearer the head of the column.

"Should not ve be going vis zem?" Karl asked Sam.

"There's no hurry," Sam told him. "Those men can't be led. They're a mob now, and a mob takes on a life of its own. If there's trouble, they'll find it without any help from us."

Sam watched the departing miners, and he shook his head. Then he walked back to where the two dead claim jumpers lay. He picked up the second man's Winchester. "Either of you ever shoot at a man before?"

Karl and Frenchy looked at each other and shook their heads. "No."

Sam pulled a dollar from his pocket and flipped it in the air. "Call it."

"Heads," said Frenchy.

Sam caught the coin, slapped it on the back of his hand and looked. "Tails." He tossed the rifle to old Karl. "Take this fellow's spare shells." He indicated the dead man.

He gave Frenchy the dead men's pistols and ammunition. "That squirrel gun won't help you much. We get to fighting up close, these'll be handier. Now we better get going."

Sam would have given anything for a hot cup of coffee. He'd have given anything for some sleep in a warm bed. His body was a mass of pain, but he had to ignore it and go back to Hastings's mine. Hastings and Egan were there, and he intended to get them. He intended to take them—or their bodies—back to Tucson and collect that reward.

The sky was heavy and the wind was raw, as the mob of miners poured up the road to Hastings's mine. They knew that road, it was easy for them to follow. In their anger and desire for food, they didn't have the inclination or the prudence to scout out a new trail, or to send out advance guards. The road took many turns, following the twisting contours of the mountain. As the miners came around the bend near the guard shack, they were greeted by a volley of rifle fire.

Men spun and fell. Others crumpled. Others staggered or dropped to their knees, crawling around in their own blood. The rest dived for the cover of the trees and snowbanks, leaving the road to the dead and wounded. To the rear, Sam and his two friends heard the firing and speeded up.

The ambushed miners tried to fight back, but Hastings's men were well positioned above them, and they kept up an accurate fire. Anyone rising up to shoot was driven back under cover by a hail of bullets. One man tried to crawl away, back around the bend, but he was hit. The miners couldn't go forward, and they couldn't go back. The cries and moans of the wounded mixed with the crack of rifles. It started to snow.

Meanwhile Sam and the others came on. "They're not moving," Sam said, listening to the gunfire. "They're pinned down. Come on."

He led Karl and Frenchy off the road, into the trees. They circled around the battle, crouching low, alert, trying to move as quietly as possible in the crusted snow. The gunfire helped cover their noise. Sam was in the lead, then Frenchy, with Karl hobbling in the rear, pipe clenched in his teeth. Sam didn't know how much use these two would be in a gunfight. He was about to find out.

They got above the gunfire, then worked over to it. From their vantage point they looked down on Hastings's men, who were well protected behind rocks, snowbanks, and folds in the ground.

Sam motioned Karl and Frenchy to spread out. They eased into firing positions, picking out targets through the falling snow. Sam had hoped to see Egan or Steele, but they weren't there. This was just a small party, put out to delay the miners' advance.

"Ready?" Sam asked.

Karl and Frenchy nodded.

"Let's do it."

Sam aimed his captured Winchester at one of the gunmen. He squeezed the trigger.

There was a bang. The gunman's head slammed into the snowbank, and he lay still. Even at this distance, Sam could see the red stain spreading beneath him. Beside Sam, Frenchy fired his pistol. The shot missed, and he swore. Then Karl fired his new rifle. His man yelped and rolled over, holding his side.

"Ha! Ha!" Karl yelled. He began jumping up and down with excitement.

"Beginner's luck," Frenchy told him sourly.

"Ha! You sink so?" Karl levered another shell into the chamber, aimed, and fired again. Another one of Hastings's men went down.

"Damn," swore Frenchy, shaking his head.

"Pour it on," Sam told them. The three of them began firing. Hastings's men were unprotected from the rear and made easy targets. They were surprised by this new attack. They couldn't hold up under it, and they broke and ran. The miners followed, yelling and firing their rifles. They tore down the bar across the road, with the sign that said: KEEP OUT.

The wounded were left where they lay, to an uncertain fate in the cold and falling snow. No one stayed to help them. The miners were motivated by more than anger and rage at Hastings—they were motivated by starvation. They knew there was food on Paradise Mountain, and they were desperate to get it—and to take revenge on those who had kept it from them.

Sam fired as long as he had a target, then he, Karl, and Frenchy got up and kept moving.

Hastings's gunmen would have stopped and ambushed the miners again, but the miners were too close on their heels. They didn't give Hastings's men time to stop and reorganize. There was skirmishing between the two groups as they struggled over the mountaintop. Sam and his friends straggled behind the battle, delayed by a series of tangled ravines, through which they were forced to work their way.

As the miners crested the ridge into the valley, they were hit by rolling waves of gunfire. Men fell, but the rest kept going, cheering and firing their weapons indiscriminately.

"They're wasting ammunition," Sam told his companions as they paused, out of breath, to listen to the battle.

Johnny Egan had warned Hastings that there might be trouble from Slater and the mob of armed miners that had driven him and his men from Karl and Frenchy's cabin. Hastings's men in the valley—both mine guards and hired claim jumpers—had been given time to prepare for this attack. They were dug in on the slopes on both sides of the stream. Their accurate fire made the lower valley a death trap, as those miners who tried to go that way found out. The rest of the miners were forced onto the slopes. They advanced slowly through the trees and rugged terrain, trading shots with Hastings's gunmen in the snow.

Behind the main line of gunmen, Hastings

stood with Egan and Steele, the captain of his mine guards. Just behind them were Steve Tracy and Marshal Jeffcoat. They watched the miners' attack lose momentum.

"There ain't enough of them to press home an attack against these positions," Steele said confidently. "The fools'll be massacred."

Harry Hastings nodded. The brim of his wide-awake hat was white with snow. "I'd prefer not to have them all dead. I need men to work my mine. Plus, there's another matter I wish to take care of. Mr. Steele, I'll have some kind of a white flag, if you please."

"A white flag!" said Steele. "But . . . "

"You heard me, Mr. Steele."

The guard captain tied a handkerchief to his rifle barrel and waved it. The gunfire began to slacken.

Johnny Egan turned to Marshal Jeffcoat. "I ain't seen Slater. I wonder where he's at."

"Maybe he got shot," Jeffcoat said.

"Anybody who could survive a fall off that mountain? It ain't likely he'll catch a bullet from this bunch. I hope not, anyway. I want him for myself."

"You'll have to get in line," said Jeffcoat grimly. He still remembered the humiliation he'd suffered when Slater had escaped from his jail.

The firing had stopped completely now. Sam, Karl, and Frenchy were just making their way to the miners' lines. The embattled miners greeted

Sam's arrival with a weak cheer.

"If they'd listened to what I said, they wouldn't be in this mess," Sam swore to himself.

Across from them, Harry Hastings suddenly appeared in the open, holding the white flag.

"Gutsy bastard, I'll give him that," Frenchy remarked.

Hastings's voice boomed. "Come on, men! There's no need for this killing. We can find a way around our differences. Let's negotiate. I'll give you all the food you want—if you give me Sam Slater."

For a moment Sam was worried, but the miners were past reasoning. One of them raised his rifle and fired at Hastings. "Negotiate with this, asshole!"

The bullet missed, and Hastings scrambled back under cover, to derisive cheers from the miners. The mine owner was furious as he brushed the snow from his expensive clothes. "The devil with them. I don't care what it costs to recruit experienced men. They had their chance. Kill them all, Mr. Steele."

Steele grinned. To his men, he said, "You heard the boss. Open fire."

Gunfire crashed. Once more the valley was wreathed in powder smoke. The miners attempted to resume their advance, but it quickly bogged down under the firepower that Hastings's men brought to bear against it. The miners were forced to take cover. Their fire dwindled. They were running out of ammunition, and their casualties were mounting.

"You should have taken my offer, boys," cried Hastings gleefully. "It's too late now."

Hastings's men redoubled their fire. The miners were becoming demoralized. Hungry and emaciated, many were so tired from the battle that they were incapable of further action. Some fell asleep where they lay.

"What can we do?" Frenchy asked Sam.

"Not much," Sam replied. "These boys bit off more than they can chew. If this snow gets heavier, maybe they can sneak off. Or maybe they can hold out till dark and leave then."

"What about you?"

"I'm staying here. I got things to do before I go."

Suddenly there was a great shout and rattle of gunfire from behind them.

"Vat is zat?" said Karl, looking over his shoulder.

"It's the reinforcements from town," Sam cried. He knew that this was the moment to strike. He jumped up and ran out in front of the oncoming miners. "Come on, men!"

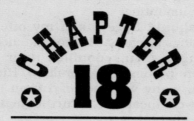

CHAPTER 18

THE OTHER MINERS ROSE BEHIND SAM—
those who were left. The new men came on with
a cheer. There were at least a hundred of them.
There were more in town and in the mountains,
but this was the first group to reach the battle.

Led by Sam, they advanced on Hastings's
men, moving through powder smoke and
swirling snow. Rifle fire riddled their ranks. Men
threw up their hands and fell, but the rest came
on, cheering and firing their weapons.

"Fall back!" Hastings ordered his men. "Fall
back!"

There was more cheering as the miners over-
ran the gunmen's positions. A few of Hastings's

men and the wounded tried to surrender, but they were shot out of hand. "No prisoners!" was the cry. Sam didn't like the summary executions, but the miners were crazed by starvation and a desire for revenge, and he could not stop them.

Sam still wore the plaid cap. It made him a better target, but he didn't care. He stopped beside a dead man and replenished his ammunition. He took the man's pistol and stuck it in his waistband. He looked for Hastings and Egan, but there was no sign of them. Between the snow and the powder smoke, visibility was down to a few feet. Figures loomed out of the murk, and it was hard to tell whether they were friend or foe. Sam thought of the wounded who had been left behind. He wondered how many would die of their wounds. He wondered how many would freeze to death before help came for them.

Karl and Frenchy were still with him. Karl had lost his pipe and hat. His eyes were wide in his smoke-blackened face. "I vish ze Austrians had fought zis vell at Sadowa," he shouted. "Ve vould have shown Mr. Bismarck and his Prussians somesing zen, by golly ve vould."

Frenchy grinned at him and shook his head. "Come on, Napoleon."

Hastings's men retreated to the mine complex, firing as they went. They took positions in the buildings and in the great stamping mill.

"Keep going," Sam yelled, leading the miners forward. Before he could get to Hastings and

Egan, their gunmen had to be overcome, position by position.

As the miners came on, they were met with a withering fire. They fought back, taking cover and pouring their own fire into the mine buildings. It was getting dark. The flashes of gun barrels winked like hundreds of deadly fireflies through the falling snow.

"Take the barracks first," Sam yelled to the miners over the gunfire and shouting.

The guards' long barracks and cookhouse stood like roadblocks before the hulking mass of the stamping mill. The miners closed in on the buildings. The cookhouse was set on fire, and its defenders retreated to the barracks.

The miners poured volley after volley into the wooden barracks, splintering walls and doors, smashing shutters and knocking them off their hinges. The rolling gunfire reverberated off the mountains. Hastings's men fought back desperately, but gradually their fire lessened.

Sam rose from the snow where he had taken position. "Now!" he yelled, waving his rifle and running forward.

With a cheer the miners rushed the barracks. There were a few last shots of defiance, then the surviving gunmen retreated out the back doors, to the foreboding mass of the stamping mill. Others were cut off and played a deadly game of hide-and-seek with the miners among the rail trestles and ore cars.

Sam was the first man inside the barracks. He could hardly see for the thick curtain of powder smoke. Dead and wounded lay everywhere, in puddles of blood. Sam hurried through the long building, checking each man. None was Hastings or Egan. Sam swore to himself. Shots sounded behind him as the miners finished off the wounded.

Sam went back outside, into the snow. Before him loomed the giant stamping mill. From inside the mill, Hastings's men fired through windows and doors. The place was a natural fortress.

"Wish we had a couple cannons," Frenchy said.

The miners advanced on the mill, but they were quickly pinned down by the fire from inside. From their five levels of elevation, Hastings's men had a perfect vantage point from which to shoot down on the attackers, who were outlined against the snow. Men were dropping by the second.

"We'll all be killed if we stay here," Sam cried. "Come on!"

Once again he led the rush forward. He was as crazed as the miners who followed him, now. All he could think about was finding Hastings and Egan. All he could think about was killing them. Above him a spark flared on the shingle roof of the mill's second floor, then died. A minute later it came back, burning strong.

Sam ran toward the smoke-shrouded stamping mill. The deepening snow tugged at his ankles. Bullets flew around him; they clutched at his already torn clothing. He reached the lower wall, by the boiler room, and dived for its cover. Frenchy, Karl, and the rest of the miners were behind him.

Sam moved along the wall, crouching as rifles were fired out the windows over his head. He rounded a corner of the boiler room, found a door, and went in.

Somewhere above him he heard the fire roaring. Smoke filled the dark room. The only illumination came from the reflected snow outside. One of Hastings's gunmen appeared before him, as if conjured up by magic. Both men fired at the same time. The gunman's shot screamed off metal. Sam's shot struck home, and the gunman fell against one of the steam boilers and slid to the floor.

Sam kept going. Behind him other miners invaded the ground floor of the huge building. Sam heard gunshots as they fought with Hastings's men. He heard muffled shouts in the smoke. He moved out of the boiler room to the second floor, following the giant conveyor belts that turned the crushers high above. He was among the settling tanks now, where the gold and silver were separated from the tailings after being cooked with mercury. The thick, acrid smoke irritated his eyes, and he rubbed them with the back of his wrist.

He was aware of movement to his left. He turned, rifle leveled, but he was not fast enough. Behind him a pistol banged twice. Through the smoke he saw a long-haired figure slump to the floor beside the huge tanks. It was Buffalo Bill.

Bill raised his head weakly from the floor.

"Hello, Sam," he said, grinning. "Sure wish you had joined our side." Then he fell back, dead.

Sam turned to see who had saved him. It was Frenchy.

"Thanks," Sam said.

"My pleasure," replied Frenchy.

Both men ducked as bullets splintered the wall beside them. They fired back, then got up and kept going, firing as shadowy targets presented themselves. More miners swept through the room holding the settling tanks, battling up to the next floor, which held the amalgamating pans, where the ore was cooked. The fire burned more fiercely now. The whole mill was in flames. The heat and smoke were intense. There was a popping sound as dried resins in the wooden beams exploded. Sam was hot and sweaty, a strange feeling after a day of combatting the cold outside.

Sam looked around. "Where's Karl?"

"Don't know," Frenchy said. "He'll be all right, though. Anybody that old and cantankerous, you can't kill him with a little battle."

The mill's machinery was enveloped in flames. Thick, oily smoke billowed through the building. It was becoming impossible to breathe.

"Can't go on," Sam swore, gasping. "We have to get out."

He and Frenchy started back the way they had come, but the passage was blocked by flames and smoke. They turned around and tried to climb higher, but there were flames that way, too. They were trapped. There was only one chance, if they were not to be burned alive.

"Come on," Sam said.

Feeling their way, because they could no longer see, they made their way down the floor. Sam touched one of the amalgamating pans and withdrew his hand with an oath. The intense heat had turned the pan's metal surface red-hot. Then he encountered a wall. They had reached the end of the passage. Blindly, Sam felt along the wall.

"You looking for a miracle?" Frenchy coughed, behind him.

"No, a window. Here, I've found one."

There was no glass in the window, only wooden shutters, which had already been knocked out by the mill's defenders. Behind Sam and Frenchy the flames drew closer. Sam felt his whiskers and eyebrows singe.

"Come on," he yelled to Frenchy.

He climbed through the window and threw himself headlong, falling into the deep snow below. Frenchy landed alongside, narrowly missing him. The two men sucked the cold, fresh air into their lungs. They rolled onto their knees, weak and coughing.

Around them the battle continued. Other men were jumping out the windows of the mill to save themselves. The flames from the burning building lit up the mountainside, turning the falling snow orange. There was fighting all over the complex. Men shot their own comrades in their blood lust and confusion. From inside the building came horrible screams as the wounded were caught by the encroaching flames. Sam wondered if Hastings and Egan were in there.

The fighting spread up the hillside, toward the cave where the food was stored. There was more fighting around the storage sheds and the ore cars. The outcome was no longer in doubt, however. With the mill gone, Hastings's position was lost.

"Which way?" Frenchy asked Sam.

Sam thought. If Hastings and Egan were not dead or in the mill, where would they be?

"Hastings's house. Come on."

They started past the mill, for the house. The company's grounds were bathed in red light from the fires. The miners were out of control, screaming like men who had gone insane. Bodies lay everywhere in the snow. The wounded crawled about or cried for help.

Near one of the trestles that carried the ore cars from the valley up to the mine shafts, Sam and Frenchy stopped. A figure dangled overhead, lit by the flickering light of the fires. It was Steele, the captain of the mine guards. The miners had captured him and lynched him from the trestle supports.

"Damn," muttered Frenchy. "These boys is gettin' hard core."

Sam tapped Frenchy's shoulder, and they kept going. They reached Hastings's two-story house. The mob hadn't been here yet—they were intent on the mountainside, and the food that was stored there. No lights shone inside the house.

Sam readied his rifle. He stepped onto the porch, with Frenchy behind. Any noise that they made was drowned out by the gunfire and yelling.

The front door was partly open. Sam could see nothing inside. "Cover me," he whispered to Frenchy.

He gripped the rifle tightly. He kicked the door all the way open and stepped in, ready to fire.

The hallway was empty.

From the parlor, just down the hall, he heard a noise. He moved silently to the door and stepped in, with Frenchy right behind.

The room was lit red by the fires outside. There were two people present—Steve Tracy and Hastings's girlfriend, the whore called the Yellow Rose. The girl gasped with fear as Sam and Frenchy came in. With one hand Tracy pointed a pistol at Sam. With the other he swept Rose protectively behind him. His carefully arranged hair had come awry over his balding head.

Sam held his fire, just barely. He knew he must be a ghastly sight, torn and bloody, the long scar on his cheek highlighted by the glare of the flames. The bandage that Laramie had put over his left eye had long since fallen off, and the cut leaked blood. He saw Rose and he thought of Laramie. He wanted the men who had killed her dead. He wanted it as badly as he had ever wanted anything.

"Where's Hastings?" he asked in a throaty voice.

"Gone," said Tracy, the pistol still pointed. "Pulled out."

"And Egan?"

"Gone with him. Jeffcoat, too. You just missed them."

Sam swore to himself. Then he said, "He didn't take his girl?"

"No." There was no hiding the contempt in Tracy's voice for his former partner.

"Why didn't you go with them?"

Tracy hesitated. He was not a man who talked about his feelings toward women, even whores. Even after what Rose had done to him, leaving him for Hastings, he couldn't let her be abandoned to the mercy of the miners. If it meant giving up his own life to save her—well, he was a man of honor, and honor sometimes required the supreme sacrifice.

"I came to offer the lady my protection, such as it is," he said.

Rose stood behind Tracy, fists clutched near her throat. She was scared of Sam, scared of the mob. She had been Hastings's girl, and because of that they were liable to do anything to her.

"How'd Hastings get away?" Sam asked.

Tracy sneered. "He has a trail out of here that only he knows. His 'bolt hole,' he calls it. He scouted it out last summer when he first came here. He's headed for town. He's either going to fort up there or take some animals from his stables and try to get below."

Sam let out his breath. He lowered the Winchester. "Go on," he told Tracy. "Get out of here. Save yourselves, before the miners come for you." He tried to think where they could go to be safe. Then he turned. "Frenchy, can they lay up at your place till this blows over?"

Frenchy grinned at the thought of the great Steve Tracy and the high-toned Yellow Rose hiding out in his cabin. "Long's they don't try to get me in no card games while they're there."

Tracy replaced his pistol in its shoulder holster. Stiffly, formally, he said, "Thank you, Mr. Slater. I—"

"Just go," Sam told him. "I don't like you, Tracy, but that's no reason to see you dead. There's been too much killing already. Anyway, I'm thinking of the girl."

Tracy nodded. He put a protective arm around Rose. "Come, my dear." Rose gave Sam and Frenchy a grateful look and turned away. The memory of her hard face stayed with Sam for a moment, but in his imagination the face had become Laramie's.

Tracy and Rose left the house. Frenchy went with them, explaining how to reach his cabin. Sam came last. Then Tracy and Rose hurried away, keeping to the shadows for safety. Sam and Frenchy watched them go, and Frenchy grinned. "You know, I wouldn't be surprised, those two didn't end up getting married."

There were still a few scattered shots around the mine complex. Above Sam and Frenchy the miners had taken the cave where the food was cached. A great mob of men had gathered there, fighting among themselves to get in, fighting over the spoils. There were screams and yells of triumph as the miners gorged themselves on the food. There was liquor in the cave, and Sam knew that the miners would be gorging themselves on that as well.

The stamping mill still burned fiercely, alight from the top floor to the bottom. Suddenly the great structure collapsed upon itself, sending billowing clouds of yellow and red and orange high into the night sky, illuminating the whole valley.

"Damn," murmured Frenchy at the sight.

The flames from the other burning buildings were dwarfed by the conflagration of the mill. The few buildings, like Hastings's house, that weren't on fire yet would soon be burned by the vengeful miners, Sam knew. By tomorrow, not a stick of this complex would be left standing.

"Where would I find Johnny Egan's cabin?" Sam asked Frenchy.

"In town, at the end of California Street. It's the last house. Why you want to know?"

Sam started away without answering.

"Wait," said Frenchy. "I'll go with you."

Sam turned. "No, you stay here and find Karl. He might be hurt and need your help. Anyway, what I have to do is best done alone."

Sam turned away and started off through the falling snow.

CHAPTER 19

THE SNOW HAD LET UP. THE RADIANT whiteness helped Sam find his way in the dark.

Sam was tired, beaten, bloody. Even his bruises had bruises. The sweat that had bathed his body and clothing in the mill was now freezing in the bitter cold, turning his shirt and trousers into garments of ice. He was starving. He wished he'd had sense enough to get some food from the mining complex. He hadn't eaten—save for one raw potato—since breakfast at Laramie's house, two days ago, and that hadn't exactly been a big meal.

He took the main road back to town. He had no idea where Hastings's secret trail was, and there was no sense trying to find it. He'd have to accept that the mine owner and his men would have a good lead on him by the time they reached town. If they left on mules and killed off the remaining stock in town—the smart thing for them to do—he would never catch them.

No, he thought. He'd catch them. He'd catch them if it took twenty years.

He passed miners still coming from their cabins to the mining complex, eager to take action against those who had kept food from them.

"What's happening back there?" they asked when they saw Sam headed the other way. "It ain't over, is it?"

"Don't sound so disappointed," Sam told them. "All you missed was the chance to get yourself killed."

He passed other men as well, the dead and wounded from both sides in the running battle. The wounded were miserable, coated with newly fallen snow. Some were moaning or crying. One man crawled along with implacable purpose, a foot at a time, in the direction of the mine. Others sat, numb with cold and shock, waiting for the inevitable. There was nothing Sam could do to help them. There were too many, and he had no time.

The road led over the mountain's crest and down into the valley, toward town. Behind Sam, a reddish-orange glow filled the night sky, from the fires at the mine.

When Sam at last crossed the river into the town, there were few men in the streets. The rest had gone to the mine. It was eerily quiet—there was no music from the saloons, no drunkard's gunshots, no laughter or cursing. This, in a town that normally went full tilt twenty-four hours a day. What little sound there was, was muffled by the falling snow. The distant glow from the burning mine gave the snow-covered buildings a rosy tinge.

Sam walked down Main Street until he came to A. Rhodes's hardware store. The door was locked. With the butt of his Winchester, Sam smashed it open and went in. Reflected light from the snow outside provided sufficient illumination. He searched beneath the gun racks for the ammunition. He opened a box of .44–40 shells and filled his pockets with them. Then he shucked off Willie's buffalo-robe coat. The coat was too small, it might get in his way. He pushed aside the broken door and went back out, headed for the river, and the Hastings Company's warehouse.

In the warehouse, Hastings, Johnny Egan, Marshal Tom Jeffcoat, and three warehouse guards were loading mules for the trip below. They had brought the mules from the company's stables, down the street. There was one string to carry food and supplies, another half-dozen to be saddled and ridden. They had killed the rest of the animals in the stables.

The men loaded heavy sacks of gold dust onto the mules' packs. The dust was from Hastings's mine. There had been more, but this was all they had been able to carry. There was also a small satchel of greenbacks, all that was left of the money Hastings had borrowed from Robinette in Tucson.

"God, I'm beat," Jeffcoat complained. "Lugging this gold from the mine really took it out of me. I ain't used to so much work."

"It was worth it, though," Hastings told him. "This way we're all leaving this place with a stake, and that's more than any of us got here with. I'd hoped to get out with millions, not thousands, but it can't be helped. We just ran into some bad luck."

"It's all Slater's fault," growled Egan. Egan still carried his baseball bat. He'd had it a long time, and he considered it not only his trademark but his good-luck charm. "We should have killed him when we had the chance, instead of trying to play it cute. If you'd let me bust his head when I did it to the girl, we'd have been all right."

Hastings loaded another sack of the gold onto his mule. "All right, Johnny, I admit it—I made a mistake. I wanted Slater's death to look plausible. I didn't want anybody asking questions. If I had to do it again, I'd do it different, but I don't have that luxury, so be happy you're getting away with your life and a nice hunk of change."

Barnes, one of the warehouse guards, said, "Lucky you had food here, Mr. Hastings. If you'd had to carry that down, you wouldn't have been able to bring the gold."

Hastings kept a secret stash of food at the warehouse. That was where his operatives in town, men like Egan and Jeffcoat, came to get theirs. When supplies ran low, more was brought down on mule back from the mine.

Jeffcoat wiped his dark brow, catching his breath. "What I don't understand is why Steve Tracy stayed back at the mine. He's gonna get his ass drilled."

"Tracy's a southerner," Hastings explained. "He's got his head full of ideas about honor and gallantry."

"Getting yourself killed is carrying gallantry kind of far," Jeffcoat said. "You don't think he's in love with Rose, do you?"

Hastings shrugged. "He probably doesn't know, himself."

"What do you think will happen to her?"

"Who cares? She's just a whore."

Egan laughed at that.

Jeffcoat said, "Maybe we should go to Steve's place and get some booze for the trip down below."

Hastings scorned that suggestion. "Booze'll kill you in the cold. Didn't you learn anything when you were a buffalo hunter?" Then he brightened, because he had an idea of his own. "But I know what you *can* go to Tracy's for."

"What?"

"The gold in his safe. He's got plenty of it, and it won't do him any good where he's going. There's no sense leaving it here for these sourdoughs, and with the mules, we can carry it."

Jeffcoat liked the idea, but he said, "How do we open the safe? Steve's the only one with the combination."

"Blow it," Hastings told him. "There's half a ton of blasting powder in the back room. Barnes'll show you where. You two do that, and we'll finish loading and saddling the mules. We'll meet you at the Metropolitan, on our way out of town."

"All right," Jeffcoat said. "Come on, Barnes."

Jeffcoat took his shotgun. The guard named Barnes led him through the cavernous warehouse into the locked back room, where they took a couple of small, flannel-wrapped powder charges and fuses to go with them. They left the warehouse and started down the street for Tracy's saloon. Then they stopped, as they saw a tall figure coming toward them.

Sam saw Jeffcoat and another man emerge from the warehouse. They were carrying what looked like powder charges and fuses. Jeffcoat wore his long black coat. Both men carried shot-guns. They stopped in surprise when they saw Sam.

Sam kept coming.

"Slater!" swore Jeffcoat. He dropped his powder and fuses to the snow, and a look of anticipation came over his well-groomed face. "No bounty hunter makes a fool of me. I'm going to fill you with more holes than a screen door."

Jeffcoat raised his shotgun; so did Barnes. But Sam's Winchester fired first. He put a bullet in Jeffcoat's chest, causing the marshal to discharge both barrels of his shotgun into the air. Another bullet sent Barnes spinning. Barnes tried to recover and fire, but two more bullets from Sam's rifle knocked him backward, and he fell dead in the snow.

Jeffcoat lay on his back. Grimacing with pain, he reached into his coat for one of his pistols. Sam fired again. Jeffcoat twitched and lay still.

"You talk too much," Sam told him.

The shooting brought a reaction from the warehouse. Pale faces appeared at the large open doors. "Jesus Christ, it's Slater!" yelled Johnny Egan.

Rifles began firing from the doorway. Sam dived and rolled in the snow as bullets spurted around him. He aimed at the doorway and squeezed off a shot. One of the warehouse guards staggered against the open door, then sank slowly down until he came to a sitting position, with his head slumped over.

The rest of the men in the warehouse kept up a hot fire at Sam, who answered in kind. The loaded mules inside brayed and kicked, then they broke loose from their tethers and ran out of the building and down the street. The men in the warehouse started after them, but they were driven back by Sam's accurate shooting. The few men who remained in town watched the battle from doorways and windows.

There was no cover in the street, so Sam hugged the ground while he reloaded his rifle from the bullets in his pockets.

From the doorway Hastings cried gleefully, "You'll have to come in after us, Slater. We're in no hurry to leave. We've got enough supplies to stay here all winter."

"Be my guest," Sam cried back. "Those miners will be back here soon, and when they come, they'll be looking for you."

He heard somebody curse from inside. Hastings and his men couldn't sneak out the back door. They had to recover the mules, which were now standing placidly up the street. The mules had the money and, more importantly, they had the supplies, without which Hastings and the others would never have a chance of getting below.

Without warning the three men charged

from the warehouse door. They spread out and advanced on Sam, shooting. Hastings and the third guard, Talbot, were firing rifles, Egan had a pistol in one hand and his baseball bat in the other, hoping he could get close enough to use it.

Sam lay flat in the snow. He ignored the bullets hitting around him and calmly fired back. The guard Talbot threw up his hands and fell on his face. Hastings was hit in the shoulder. He stopped advancing and fired a few more shots, one-handed. Then he took another bullet in the side, and he and Egan retreated into the warehouse.

The street was suddenly quiet. Wisps of powder smoke drifted away on the breeze. Hastings and Egan were in the warehouse, regrouping, trying to think of another way out. Sam had them now. All he had to do was wait for the miners to return. He wouldn't have to fire another shot; he wouldn't have to lift a finger. The miners would take care of Hastings and Egan for him.

But Sam didn't want the miners to kill Hastings and Egan. He remembered what Hastings and Egan had done to Laramie. He wanted to kill them himself. He rose and moved forward.

He kept his eyes on the warehouse doors, but no one appeared there. As he approached the huge building he braced himself and dived inside the doors, exposing himself against the entrance for as short a period as possible. Two shots sounded as he dived in, but both missed, splintering wood above him.

He lay there, catching his breath, trying to make out where Hastings and Egan were. He'd seen their muzzle flashes, but he'd heard movement as they shifted their positions after firing. The only illumination in the warehouse was provided by the snow reflected through the open front doors. There were no windows and all the lanterns had been extinguished. In the dark interior Sam saw enormous crates of machinery, spare parts, conveyor belts, wagons, wheels, ore cars—all the items needed to construct and run a mining operation. In the open doorway were splashes of blood that led to the rear.

"Come on, Slater!" It was Hastings's voice, taunting, from the blackness deep inside the building. There was pain in the voice, and Sam knew he was hurt. "Come and get us. We're waiting for you."

Sam figured they were hiding among the crates and machinery, hoping to catch him in a cross fire as he came to them. He was ready to take that chance.

Then he remembered something else that was stored in the warehouse.

On his hands and knees Sam crawled back out the door. There were no shots. Maybe they hadn't seen him, or maybe they thought he was scared and running away. Maybe they thought it was a trick to get them to fire and reveal their positions. Once in the street, he stood and ran back to where Jeffcoat and Barnes lay. He picked up the bags of blasting powder, leaving the fuses. He had to be quick, before Hastings and Egan figured out what he was up to and got out of the building.

Sam guessed that the main supply of blasting powder was kept at the rear of the warehouse. He ran back that way, silent in the new snow. With his knife he punched a hole in one of the powder bags. Then he ran a line of powder to the rear of the building. He placed both bags at the end of the powder line, against the building wall. He ran back. Cupping his hand against the wind, he struck a match. The flame sputtered, then took hold. He laid it to the end of the powder train. There was a puff of smoke and a spark. Sam took off, getting the hell out of the way.

The spark ate up the powder train, running across the snow to the back of the building. The spark reached the powder bags. There were two explosions, followed a second later by a series of tremendous blasts that rippled through the warehouse, as over a half ton of blasting powder went up, barrel by barrel.

The warehouse was blown apart. The roof, pieces of wood and machinery, and who knew what else went flying into the night air, along with a dense column of smoke and flame. The debris rained back down, thudding into the snow. Sam huddled beside a building, arms over his head protectively.

When Sam looked up, the warehouse was an inferno. Smaller explosions continued to go off inside, bright sparks of color against the roiling smoke. Pieces of wood and debris skyrocketed into the air.

"Looks like Fourth of July came early," he muttered to himself.

Then he sighed. He couldn't take Hastings and Egan back to Tucson now. There wouldn't be enough left of them. He had the documents stolen from Robinette's house as evidence of what he had accomplished, but he wanted additional proof that he had earned all three thousand dollars of the reward.

He rose and started down the debris-strewn street. Men had come out of their hiding places and were staring at the burning warehouse in awe. In addition, the miners who had attacked the Hastings mine complex were drifting back. Many were drunk. They had begun looting the shops and saloons. There were random gunshots. A fire had started, whether by one of the miners or as a by-product of the warehouse explosion, Sam didn't know. Borne on the wind, the fire spread from building to building, but no one seemed to care.

Sam turned and walked to the end of California Street. According to Frenchy, the last cabin on the street was Johnny Egan's. The cabin was more of a shack, ill built and dirty, with empty tin cans all around the outside. Sam went in. Even with the bitter cold, he wrinkled his nose against the smell. He couldn't imagine what the place must be like in the heat of summer. He looked around. There wasn't much inside—some clothing on the floor, extra boots, a couple of guns. Whiskey bottles, both full and empty. The bed was crudely made of pine slats, with filthy, yellow-brown sheets that looked like they'd never been washed.

Sam pulled the bed aside. Beneath it, on the packed dirt floor, was an ornamental wooden box, painted with a Navajo design and lacquered—stolen from Lord only knew where.

There was no lock on the box, and Sam opened it. Egan seemed to have been the kind of man who kept mementos of his crimes and his victims—there were articles of jewelry, money clips, even someone's gold tooth—items that Egan had no use for, but with which, for his own perverted reasons, he did not wish to part. And right on top was a silver Seth Thomas watch. Sam turned the watch over. The inscription read: "To Edward Robinette, a Loving Husband. From Melissa, on his 40th Birthday. Oct. 14, 1876."

Sam looked sadly at the watch. Now he had his additional proof—and he had something to return to Robinette's wife, Melissa.

He started to put the watch in his pocket

when he heard a noise and turned.

Johnny Egan stood in the cabin's doorway, holding his sawed-off baseball bat in one hand and a pistol in the other, and grinning.

"Breaking and entering, Slater. You could get in big trouble for that."

CHAPTER 20

SAM TRIED TO CONCEAL HIS SHOCK AT SEE-
ing Egan alive. Egan's clothes and face were
scorched and darkened.

"Take that pistol out of your belt," Egan told
Sam. "Toss it over here. Easy."

Sam did as he was told. "I thought you went
up in smoke," he said.

Egan's grin widened. "You think I'd stick
around and be killed with that fool Hastings? I
know when it's time to cut my losses, Slater.
Hastings was done for, either way. Sure, and it
served him right, for thinking he was so damn
smart. Me, I sneaked out a side door just before
the blast. Afterward, I saw you leaving the area,

and I followed you. I was going to kill you right off, but I got curious about where you was going. And what do I find? That you was coming here, to sample the poor hospitality of my own house. But that's all right. I had to come back, anyway, and get my souvenir box. Seems like you had the same idea."

Sam was still on his knees. "I needed proof that you killed Ed Robinette," he explained, setting aside the silver watch. "That's the fellow in Tucson, in case you ain't big on names."

"I know who Robinette was."

"I came to Paradise Mountain to collect the reward on his killer."

"Pity you ain't going to be successful."

Sam tried to sound bored. "You going to shoot me, or talk me to death?"

"Neither." Egan waved the baseball bat menacingly. "I got something special planned for you. First I got to figure out what my little souvenir of you is going to be. Maybe I'll cut your cheek off, the one with the scar. I can dry it and stretch it on a little hoop, like the Injuns do with scalps. Yeah, that might look nice. 'Sam Slater's scar'—has kind of a ring to it, don't you think?"

"I'm scared," Sam deadpanned.

Egan smiled easily, a man in control. "You'll be the fifty-first notch on this bat. Robinette was forty-nine. And you see this last notch, the new one? You know who that's for? Your girlfriend, Laramie. Oh, I had fun with her, but you saw her after, so you know that. It took me a while to clean all the hair and bone off. . . . "

Sam went crazy. He exploded off the floor and threw himself at Egan. Egan's gun went off, but in his surprise the bullet only grazed Sam's cheek. The two men wrestled against the wall, then Egan kneed Sam's groin and sent him reeling.

Egan looked at Sam, grinning openmouthed, like some huge, predatory animal. He tossed his pistol away contemptuously, and he came on with the sawed-off baseball bat. "I'm going to enjoy this," he said.

Egan feinted with the bat, and Sam stepped back. Egan feinted again. He and Sam waltzed around the little cabin. A third feint, and Sam moved backward, bumping into the bed. He looked behind him involuntarily. As he did, Egan swung the bat. Sam managed to block the blow with his arm, but the bat caught him on the point of the elbow.

"Ow!" Sam yelled. Pain shot up and down his arm. Then the arm went numb, and useless, from his elbow to his fingertips. Egan laughed and swung the bat again, two-handed, this time, with all his strength behind it. Sam turned away, trying to duck the blow, but it caught him across the back. He cried with agony and sank to his knees.

As Egan lifted the bat again, Sam desperately lurched to his left and with his good hand grabbed the big man around the ankles. Off bal-

ance, Egan aimed his blow downward, trying to
break Sam's spine, but he missed by a little bit
and hit Sam on the hip instead.

Summoning all his strength into his good arm,
Sam twisted, throwing Egan to the ground. He fell
on top of Egan, and the two men rolled around on
the tiny floor. They banged into the bed, knocking
it back against the wall. Egan jabbed the knob of
the bat into Sam's face, stunning him.

Egan scrambled to his feet, drawing the bat
back for the killing blow. Sam came after, giving
him no time to swing. Sam put his head down
and bulled into Egan's gut, knocking him across
the floor and through the flimsy cabin wall, into
the snow outside, lit red by the fires raging
through the town.

Egan tried to get up. Sam threw his left shoulder, the numb one, into him, knocking him back
down. In the light from the fires, Sam saw an old
tin-can lid nearby. With his good hand he reached
out, grabbed the jagged lid, and jabbed it through
Egan's beard, into his neck. The rusty metal bit
deep. Sam grabbed it tightly, feeling the metal cut
through what was left of the glove on his hand
and not caring. While Egan struggled beneath
him, he sawed the lid back and forth across the
big man's neck, severing his jugular vein.

Shock came into Egan's piggish eyes. The
jagged line across his throat turned red, and suddenly blood spurted out. It flooded through his
beard, down his neck, and over his chest. Egan

grabbed at the wound as though trying to push the blood back in. He tried to talk but only gurgled.

Sam leaned in close to Egan's face, making sure that the big man heard. "That's for Laramie," he said.

Egan was choking on his own blood. It was pouring out, splashing onto the snow. He tried to stand up. He got halfway, began flailing wildly with his arms, and collapsed. He looked up at Sam in anguish. Then the light in his eyes dimmed and went out. He fell on his face.

Sam dropped the rusty lid. He plunged his hand into the snow, to clean and numb it and try to stop the bleeding. Then he walked away from Egan's body. He went back into the cabin and put Robinette's silver watch in his pocket. He took his pistol from the floor and started back toward Main Street. The feeling had started to return to his left arm. The feeling was pain. He wished to hell the arm had stayed numb.

On Main Street the fire had spread. The whole town of Paradise Mountain was being consumed. The Metropolitan was on fire, and Sam heard breaking glass as somebody smashed the long mirror. The Through Ticket was in flames as well. Charley's would be going up at any minute. Down by the river the warehouse still burned, though the thudding explosions had ceased. The town's population seemed to have lost its collective reason. Drunken men were looting the buildings. They were shooting into the air, shooting at each other. Others were leaving the buildings just ahead of the fire—carrying their possessions, or stealing someone else's. Above the noise rose screams from the whores at the Metropolitan and on the Line.

The mules with which Hastings and his men had hoped to escape still wandered Main Street. Drunken miners had discovered the gold dust in their packs. They were whooping, shouting, fighting over the gold. One sack of dust had ripped open. The precious yellow metal spilled onto the snow, then was blown down the street by the wind while men struggled to recover it. Other men rolled around in the sooty snow, punching and kicking each other in their desire to possess the gold.

Sam ignored the action around him. He picked the three likeliest mules, one packed with supplies, two saddled for riding. He checked the provisions loaded on the supply mule—grain for the animal, bread, bacon, sugar, and coffee. They would do. The gold had already been removed. That was all right, too; gold would have weighed him down, and weight was going to be a critical factor if he was to make it below.

A drunken miner grabbed his arm. "Hey, who said you could—"

Sam cocked the pistol and pointed it in the miner's face. "Nobody had to."

The miner swallowed and backed off. "Sure. Sure, mister."

Sam led the three mules back to Egan's

cabin. With difficulty, using his good arm, he heaved Egan's body onto one of the saddle mules and lashed it down.

"Sam!"

It was Frenchy, running up, carrying a rifle that he must have gotten at Hastings's mine.

"What are you doing here?" Sam asked him.

"Same as always. Come to see if you need help." The black man was out of breath. He must have run most of the way.

"Where's Karl?" Sam said, and then his stomach turned. "Jesus, he's not. . . ?"

Frenchy grinned, his big teeth reddish in the light of the fires. "No, Karl's all right. It was too far for him to run on them itty-bitty legs. He stayed behind, getting together the few what ain't lost their heads, and helping the wounded." Frenchy eyed Egan's blood-soaked body. "You kill him?"

Sam nodded.

Frenchy whistled. "Damn. What you doing now?"

"Leaving. I got what I came for."

"In this weather? You'll never make it, man."

"I'll take my chances. It's better than staying here." Sam looked around once, taking in the fires, the shooting, the screams. "Why don't you and Karl come, too?"

Frenchy considered the possibility, then dismissed it. "We'll make out all right. I'd hate to give up a good claim. Gold *is* where you find it, you know."

"What will you do? This town's destroying itself."

"We'll hunker up in our cabin till spring, I guess, us and our distinguished guests. It shouldn't be hard—we got us plenty of food now."

Sam nodded. He mounted the riding mule. Frenchy stuck up a hand. "Good luck, bounty hunter."

"Luck to you, too, Frenchy," said Sam. "You still don't look very French to me."

"I must be from the south of France. They say there's lots of sun there. Turns folks real dark."

Sam laughed. "Say good-bye to Karl for me."

"I will, when he lets me get a word in edgewise."

Sam rode out of town, leading the mules. At the head of the pass he halted and looked back. Flames ran up and down the snow-blanketed valley. Their reflections flickered on the mountainsides, which echoed with gunfire, yells, and screams.

Sam dismounted. With his knife he changed the sign at the head of the pass, crossing out the words "Paradise Mountain" and carving one of his own. Then he remounted and rode on, leading the pack mule and the mule with Johnny Egan's body.

Behind him, the sign now read:

WELCOME TO HELL

Dale Colter is the pseudonym of a full-time writer who lives in Maryland with his family.

VALLEY OF WILD HORSES
0-06-100221-6 $3.95

WILDERNESS TREK
0-06-100260-7 $3.99

THE VANISHING AMERICAN
0-06-100295-X $3.99

CAPTIVES OF THE DESERT
0-06-100292-5 $3.99

THE SPIRIT OF THE BORDER
0-06-100293-3 $3.99

BLACK MESA
0-06-100291-7 $3.99

ROBBERS' ROOST
0-06-100280-1 $3.99

UNDER THE TONTO RIM
0-06-100294-1 $3.99

**For Fastest Service–
Visa & MasterCard
Holders Call
1-800-331-3761**
